"Jesus," Sheriff Evans said, "the Gunsmith in my town. If word gets out, there'll be blood in the streets."

"You're bein' too dramatic, Sheriff," Doc Jacobs said.

"Am I? What do you think will happen if word gets out he was here?"

"I don't know."

"Gunmen will come out of the woodwork," Evans said, "that's what. How long is he stayin'?"

"I don't know."

"Well, how bad is he hurt?"

"I don't want to feed into your drama," Jacobs said.

"What do you mean?"

"At the moment," Doc Jacobs said, "the Gunsmith can't move his hand."

Evans stared at Jacobs.

"Sheriff?"

"Huh? Oh, uh, you mean . . . his gun hand?"

"That's what I mean," Jacobs said. "The puncture wound in his arm has affected the motor functions of his hand."

"Doc!"

"Like I said," Jacobs replied, "he can't use his right hand."

"Jesus!" Evans said. "If *this* gets out, we'll be drowning in gunnies."

"Why would it get out?" the doctor said. "I'm not going to tell anyone. Are you?"

DON'T MISS THESE
ALL-ACTION WESTERN SERIES
FROM THE BERKLEY PUBLISHING GROUP

THE GUNSMITH by J. R. Roberts
Clint Adams was a legend among lawmen, outlaws, and ladies. They called him . . . the Gunsmith.

LONGARM by Tabor Evans
The popular long-running series about Deputy U.S. Marshal Custis Long—his life, his loves, his fight for justice.

SLOCUM by Jake Logan
Today's longest-running action Western. John Slocum rides a deadly trail of hot blood and cold steel.

BUSHWHACKERS by B. J. Lanagan
An action-packed series by the creators of Longarm! The rousing adventures of the most brutal gang of cutthroats ever assembled—Quantrill's Raiders.

DIAMONDBACK by Guy Brewer
Dex Yancey is Diamondback, a Southern gentleman turned con man when his brother cheats him out of the family fortune. Ladies love him. Gamblers hate him. But nobody pulls one over on Dex . . .

WILDGUN by Jack Hanson
The blazing adventures of mountain man Will Barlow—from the creators of Longarm!

TEXAS TRACKER by Tom Calhoun
J.T. Law: the most relentless—and dangerous—manhunter in all Texas. Where sheriffs and posses fail, he's the best man to bring in the most vicious outlaws—for a price.

THE GUNSMITH

354

CROSS DRAW

J. R. ROBERTS

JOVE BOOKS, NEW YORK

THE BERKLEY PUBLISHING GROUP
Published by the Penguin Group
Penguin Group (USA) Inc.
375 Hudson Street, New York, New York 10014, USA
Penguin Group (Canada), 90 Eglinton Avenue East, Suite 700, Toronto, Ontario M4P 2Y3, Canada
(a division of Pearson Penguin Canada Inc.)
Penguin Books Ltd., 80 Strand, London WC2R 0RL, England
Penguin Group Ireland, 25 St. Stephen's Green, Dublin 2, Ireland (a division of Penguin Books Ltd.)
Penguin Group (Australia), 250 Camberwell Road, Camberwell, Victoria 3124, Australia
(a division of Pearson Australia Group Pty. Ltd.)
Penguin Books India Pvt. Ltd., 11 Community Centre, Panchsheel Park, New Delhi—110 017, India
Penguin Group (NZ), 67 Apollo Drive, Rosedale, North Shore 0632, New Zealand
(a division of Pearson New Zealand Ltd.)
Penguin Books (South Africa) (Pty.) Ltd., 24 Sturdee Avenue, Rosebank, Johannesburg 2196,
South Africa

Penguin Books Ltd., Registered Offices: 80 Strand, London WC2R 0RL, England

This is a work of fiction. Names, characters, places, and incidents either are the product of the author's imagination or are used fictitiously, and any resemblance to actual persons, living or dead, business establishments, events, or locales is entirely coincidental.

CROSS DRAW

A Jove Book / published by arrangement with the author

PRINTING HISTORY
Jove edition / June 2011

Copyright © 2011 by Robert J. Randisi.
Cover illustration by Sergio Giovine.

ISBN: 978-0-515-14955-5

JOVE®
Jove Books are published by The Berkley Publishing Group,
a division of Penguin Group (USA) Inc.,
375 Hudson Street, New York, New York 10014.
JOVE® is a registered trademark of Penguin Group (USA) Inc.
The "J" design is a trademark of Penguin Group (USA) Inc.

PRINTED IN THE UNITED STATES OF AMERICA

10 9 8 7 6 5 4 3 2 1

ONE

When the left rear wheel went, Rosemary Collins wondered what else could go wrong.

"What happened?" Abigail asked from the back of the covered wagon.

Rosemary leaned over to take a look. Sure enough, the wheel was lying on its side, the wagon leaning to the left.

"Everybody out!" she called.

"What?" Abigail's voice grated on her. The other girls simply got out of the wagon without comment, but Abigail bitched the entire time.

All five women stood and stared down at the wheel.

"What happened?" Jenny, the youngest, asked.

"I'm not sure," Rosemary said, "but at least the wheel isn't broken."

"Is the axle broken?" Delilah asked.

Rosemary bent over to look and said, "I hope not."

"How could we have left St. Louis without somebody who knew what they're doing?" Abigail demanded.

The other four women ignored her. It had taken them weeks, but they'd finally come to an agreement that this was the best way to handle her.

"I think that thing that holds the wheel on broke," Rosemary said, pointing. "If we could lift the wagon we could put the wheel back on. Then we'd just have to slide something in this hole to hold it on."

"Something like what?" Abigail asked.

Rosemary got down on one knee.

"A piece of wood. We just have to slide it into this hole."

"You don't know what you're doin'," Abigail said.

"I'm trying to figure it out, Abigail." Rosemary stood up. "At least I'm being constructive. All you're doing is complaining."

Abigail, the oldest of the five women, crossed her arms and pouted at being criticized.

"What can we do?" Jenny asked.

"We have to figure out a way to raise the wagon," Rosemary said, "then figure out how to slide the wheel on. And finally, how to get it to stay on."

"Oh my god," Abigail said.

"We're lucky the wheel enclosed by an iron rim," Rosemary said. "It kept the wood from snapping."

Rosemary looked at the four other women—Abigail, Jenny, Delilah, and Morgan. She was going to have to assign each a task and hope that, by working together, they could get the wagon fixed.

Because they were out in the middle of the Arizona nowhere.

* * *

Clint spotted the group from a ways off. His intention was to skirt around them and mind his own business. However, when he got to the top of a hill, he was close enough to notice two things. One, there were five women and no men in sight. Two, they had a broken wheel.

"Damn it, Eclipse," he said to his big Darley Arabian. "Can't very well ride right by them, can we?"

The Darley nodded his big head.

"Yeah, maybe you can ride by them," he said, "but I can't."

Clint directed Eclipse down the hill, toward the covered wagon and the five women who were, apparently, traveling alone.

"Rosemary!"

She turned at the sound of Jenny's voice, and the panic in it.

"Delilah," she said, "get me the rifle."

Delilah ran to the back of the wagon, took out the Winchester, and passed it to Rosemary. She held it in both hands, not pointing it but holding it at the ready as the man came toward them.

"Who is that?" Abigail asked.

They ignored her.

"What does he want?" she demanded.

They ignored her.

"What are you waiting for, Rosemary?" she asked. "Shoot him!"

"Shut up, Abigail."

"What?"

Rosemary turned to the older woman and shouted, "Shut the hell up!"

Abigail subsided into shocked silence and the five women watched the mounted man approach.

TWO

Clint advanced toward the five women, warily eyeing the one holding the rifle. She looked like she knew how to use it.

The women were of varying ages. The one holding the rifle looked to be in her early thirties. Two of the others looked older, and two younger. Three of the women looked frightened. One—the oldest—looked more annoyed than anything else. The face of the one with the rifle was impassive. Lovely, but impassive.

When he reached them, he was careful to keep both hands in view.

"You ladies look like you need some help," he said.

"That depends," Rosemary said.

"On what?" he asked.

"On what you want in return for your assistance?" she asked.

"Nothing," he said. "I see five women in need of help, I stop."

"Just out of the goodness of your heart?" the older woman asked.

"Well, actually," Clint said, "because it's the right and decent thing to do."

The older woman rolled her eyes.

The remaining three were looking toward the one with the rifle, waiting for her to make a decision.

"I don't think the axle is broke, and the wheel is still intact," she said.

"The carter key probably broke, and the wheel slipped off," Clint said. "May I dismount to have a look?"

Rosemary hesitated, then said, "Please."

"Rosemary!" the older woman said. "We don't know who he is!"

"Abigail—"

"She's right," Clint said, dismounting. "My name is Clint Adams, ladies."

"I'm Rosemary," the woman with the rifle said. "This is Jenny, Delilah, Abigail, and Morgan."

"Sisters?" Clint asked.

"Not related," Rosemary said. "We're just traveling together."

"I see."

"That's a beautiful horse," Jenny said, moving toward Eclipse.

"Be careful," Clint warned. "He doesn't usually like people."

Jenny rubbed Eclipse's nose and he leaned into it.

"He's a sweetie," she said.

"Well," Clint said, "in that case, maybe you'd like to hold his reins?"

"Sure," she said eagerly.

Clint handed Eclipse's reins over to the girl and walked to the wagon. Rosemary went with him, and they knelt down together.

"Yeah, it's the carter key," he said. "We'll have to find a way to lift the wagon and put the wheel back on, then find a replacement for the key."

"That's what I said," Rosemary commented, "only I didn't know it was called a carter key."

"The one we'll use as a replacement won't last very long," he said. "You'll have to get to the nearest town and have a real one put on."

"O-okay," she said. "Where's the nearest town?"

"Up ahead about ten miles."

"Will it last that long?"

"I don't know," he said. "I could ride along with you to make sure you make it, but we can talk about that after we get it fixed."

"How do we do that?"

"We need something to use as a lever, and something as a fulcrum."

"Are you an engineer?"

"No," he said, "but I've known some, and I've seen it done."

They stood up, Clint rubbing his hands together to clean the dirt off. He noticed that Rosemary was holding the rifle in a more relaxed manner.

"I was about to assign tasks," she said.

"Good idea," he said. "You might also put that rifle away."

She looked at the rifle then said, "Of course."

She walked around and put the rifle back in the wagon.

"Rosemary!" Abigail snapped.

"Shut up, Abigail!"

The older woman fell silent again.

"She's our complainer," Rosemary explained.

"There's one in every group," he told her. "Okay, you want to assign—"

"You can do it," she said.

"Okay, ladies," he said, "listen up. I'm going to tell you each what we need, and then you're going to go out and find it."

THREE

They needed some stones to use as a fulcrum. One large boulder would have been best, but there was no way they'd be able to carry one to the wagon. They were going to have to stack a bunch of stones to make one big one.

Then they needed a thick enough tree branch to use as a lever. And it had to be strong enough to take the wagon's weight.

He sent the women out by twos to find those things. When they returned, they all gathered near the wagon with the supplies.

First they built a small mound of stones, stacking it so that they would sit firmly and take the weight.

Next he had to find some way to get a branch free of the tree. They had no saw, and it was too thick to break off.

"How are we going to get it down?" Rosemary asked.

"Well," Clint said, hands on his hips as he considered the problem, "I guess we'll have to shoot it down."

"How do we do that?" Rosemary asked.

"It would help if we had a shotgun," Clint said. "I'd just fire at the elbow, where the branch meets the tree, try to shred it. I'll have to try it with a rifle."

"Wait," Rosemary said.

She walked to the wagon, reached in and came out with an old Greener shotgun. She carried it, with some extra shells, back to Clint.

"Twelve-gauge," Clint said. "Is it loaded?"

"Both barrels."

He broke it open to check anyway. It was loaded.

"Okay," he said. "Everybody stand back. There may be some ricochet."

The women stepped back. Clint aimed the shotgun at the tree, fired both barrels. The tree shredded. He reached up and pulled, putting his weight on the branch, bounced up and down with it. There was a crack, but the branch didn't come loose.

Jenny came over. She was the youngest, but carried more weight than the other women.

"Let me help," she said. "Maybe God made me fat for a reason."

"You're not fat, Jenny," Clint said.

"Thank you," she said, "but I'm heavier than the others."

"Well," he said, "I'll accept your help, but I still say you're not fat."

He reached up and pulled the branch down so that she could also grab hold, and then they both added their weight to the branch. Just when he thought he might have to fire again, there was a loud *crack* and the branch came free. They fell to the ground, the branch on top of them.

"You okay?" he asked.

"I'm fine," she said with a smile. "We did it."

"Thanks to you," he said. "Come on. Let's carry it over to the wagon."

Rosemary added a hand and they hauled the makeshift lever to the wagon, where their fulcrum was waiting.

"You think this is going to work?" Rosemary asked.

"I hope so."

They wedged the thick branch underneath the wagon.

"Four of you will have to put your weight on it," he said. "I need one person to help me with the wagon."

"Delilah," Rosemary said, "you're the strongest."

She was the tallest and sturdiest looking, so Clint depended on Rosemary to know her people.

"Now we need to find a replacement for the carter key."

"How do we do that?"

"Wait here," Clint said. "I'll look around."

They needed something that would fit through the hole on the hub—a thick piece of wood, or even the right-shaped stone.

He walked off, eyes cast down at the ground, looking for something that would work. Behind him, some of the women also started to look. Abigail sat down and sulked. Delilah stood by the makeshift lever and fulcrum.

"This is never gonna work," Abigail said. "We're going to die here."

"Oh, be quiet, Abigail," Delilah said. "Mr. Adams will help us get out of here."

"And then what? He'll rape us."

"All of us?" Delilah asked.

"Why not?" Abigail asked. "He's a man."

"I think we'd be able to defend ourselves against one man, Abigail," Delilah said. "Besides, he's not that kind of man."

"What makes you say that?"

"He stopped to help us, didn't he?"

Abigail stared at Delilah and then said, "Oh, don't tell me you're lusting after him."

"Abigail!"

"God," Abigail said, "one handsome man stops to help us and you act like a harlot."

"Abigail," Delilah said, "I swear, if you don't shut up . . ."

Rosemary came up alongside Clint and asked, "Will this do?"

Clint looked at what she held in her hand. It was a branch that looked the right width and length. He took it from her, held it in both hands and tried to break it. If it had been longer, he might have succeeded. The length— or lack thereof—made it stronger.

"Let's try it," he said. "Good find."

They walked back to the wagon, gathered all the other women around.

"All right," Clint said. "When I've wedged the lever underneath the wagon, four of you will put your weight on it. Once you lift the wagon up high enough, you'll have to hold it there. Understand?"

They all nodded, except for Abigail. But that was okay. They didn't need her enthusiasm, just her weight.

Clint looked at Rosemary. "You're going to help me

lift the wheel up and slide it on. Then you'll just have to hold it in place while I slide the carter key on." He held up the branch she'd found.

"Okay."

"Are we ready?" he asked the women.

They nodded.

"Okay," he said. "Put all your weight on the lever . . . now!"

They did. The wagon creaked, groaned a bit, and then lifted.

"Just a little more."

The ladies leaned harder, even Abigail on the end. The branch made a sound, but held.

"Let's lift the wheel," he told Rosemary.

They picked the wheel up, straightened it, then lifted it to put it back on. They got it onto the hub, but it wouldn't sit straight.

"Hold on!"

He left Rosemary to hold the wheel. He had the make-shift carter key in his left hand, reached behind with his right, placing his arm beneath the wagon. He reached behind to try to steady the wheel, then slid the carter key into the hole with his left. It went in, and stopped part of the way. That was good. It was big enough to wedge in there. He pushed harder so that it did just that.

"That's . . . almost . . . got it," he said.

Abigail heard him say, ". . . got it . . ." She said, "Good," and took her weight off the branch.

Without her weight the other women couldn't hold it and the wagon came down hard . . . trapping Clint's right arm beneath it.

FOUR

"Oh my God!" Rosemary shouted. "Lift it, lift it. He's trapped."

The pain was intense as something metal beneath the wagon punched into Clint's arm. He yelled again in pain.

"Abigail!" Delilah yelled.

"It's not my fault!"

"Just get back on it!" Jenny yelled.

The women leaned on the lever again, lifting the wagon. Whatever had stabbed into Clint's arm caused pain and further damage as it slid out. There was a spurt of blood and then the pain was so bad he passed out.

"Oh my God," Rosemary said again.

His blood soaked her, but she managed to get her arms around his waist and pull him out from beneath the wagon.

"I've got him! I've got him!"

The women let the wagon come back down and then rushed to see how Clint was.

"Oh, god, his arm," Jenny said.

"There's so much blood," Delilah said.

"How bad is it?" Morgan asked.

"We've got to stop the bleeding," Rosemary said. "Then we'll be able to tell."

She turned around and looked at the women. "I need a belt, some water, and some bandages. Hurry, girls!"

They scattered, even Abigail moving quickly.

Rosemary got Clint onto his back and began tearing off the right sleeve of his shirt. The wound looked ragged, but there was so much blood she couldn't tell. She knew she had to stop the bleeding somehow. She removed his gun belt, then the belt of his trousers. She wrapped the belt around his right upper arm, pulled it tight, and held it that way. That seemed to stanch the blood flow. She maintained her hold on the belt until one of the other girls returned. It was Jenny, with a belt; but since Rosemary had already pressed Clint's own belt into service, she had Jenny hold the spare.

Morgan returned with a bucket of water and some strips of cloth for bandages. Rosemary soaked some of the rags and used them to clean the wound. It was a deep puncture, and the edges were ragged. The belt had slowed the bleeding, so she packed the wound as best she could with some rags, then used the rest to wrap it tightly.

"Let the belt loose, then tighten it again," Rosemary said. "We'll have to keep doing that until the bleeding stops."

"What if it doesn't stop?" Jenny asked.

"Then he'll bleed to death before we can get him some help."

"Help where?" Morgan asked.

"He told me there's a town about ten miles ahead."

"If the wheel stays on that long," Delilah said.

"If it doesn't," Rosemary said, "one of us will take one of the team—or Mr. Adams's horse—and ride ahead for help. For now, we need to get him into the back of the wagon."

While Jenny continued to hold the belt on Clint's arm, Morgan, Delilah, and Rosemary picked Clint up and carried him to the wagon. Thankfully, he was still out, so they didn't have to worry about causing him any pain.

With difficulty, they lifted him into the back of the wagon. Eventually, Jenny got in the back and lifted his head onto her lap. She would remain in charge of the belt on his arm as long as possible. After settling him in, the girls tied Eclipse to the back of the wagon.

"Okay," Rosemary said, "let's get going and see if this wheel holds up."

Rosemary climbed up to take the reins. Abigail decided to sit next to her. Morgan also sat with them, and Delilah climbed into the back. There was plenty of room so that she didn't crowd the prone Clint. They started off, expecting with every foot they traveled to hear a crack from the wheel.

FIVE

The wheel held.

The town they came to was called Big Rock. It was a decent-sized town, and Rosemary was hopeful it had a doctor.

She stopped in front of the sheriff's office, because it seemed right to ask him.

"Stay here, all of you," she said.

She walked to the door and knocked.

"Come in!"

She entered, saw a man standing by a potbellied stove with a coffeepot in his hand. He was tall and fairly young—in his thirties—and had a pleasant, open face

"You're a stranger in town," he said. "Nobody else would knock. What can I do for you?"

"We have an injured man in our wagon, Sheriff," she said. "Is there a doctor in town?"

He put the pot down, grabbed his hat, and said, "Yes. How was he injured?"

"He stopped to help us repair our wagon wheel, and the wagon came down on his arm."

The lawman took his gun belt from a drawer in his desk and strapped it on. "Come on. I'll show you where the doctor is."

"Thank you."

He not only showed her where the doctor's office was, but he got some men to carry Clint—who was finally conscious—into the office.

He had woken up along the way and looked up at Jenny.

"What happened?"

"You got hurt," she said. "Your arm."

He looked down at his bloody right arm and started to try to move it but was stopped by the pain.

"Don't try to move," she said.

"How bad is it?" he asked.

"We're taking you to a doctor."

He remained quiet the rest of the way and gritted his teeth only once when the men carried him into the doctor's examining room and put him on a table.

"All right," Doctor Sam Jacobs announced to everybody in the room, "everyone out, now! Let me see to my patient."

The men left easily. The women lingered, but the doctor finally shooed them out.

"All right, Mr. Adams," the doctor said to Clint. "Let me have a look."

He unwrapped the wound, inspected it silently.

"How bad is it, Doc?" Clint asked.

"I don't know yet," the doctor said. "It will take some time."

"Doc," Clint said, "I can't move my fingers."

Outside the office, the women divvied up their tasks with help from the sheriff.

"I'll get us hotel rooms," Rosemary said. "Jenny, you take Clint's horse to the livery."

"Right."

"The rest of you, find someplace safe to put our wagon. It has all our possessions in it."

"I'll show you where the hotel is. The best one in town."

"Maybe," she said, "you better show me the cheapest one in town."

He laughed and they started walking.

"I don't know your name, Sheriff," Rosemary said.

"It's Evans," he said. "Cal Evans."

"Cal?"

"Calvin," the sheriff admitted, "but I don't use the whole name. What's yours?"

"Rosemary Collins," she said.

"And the man with the wound?" he asked. "I heard you call him Clint."

"Yes."

"Clint what?"

"Adams," she said, "Clint Adams. He came riding up on us early today and helped us to fix the wheel."

The sheriff stopped walking.

"Wait. Clint Adams?"

"That's right."

"The Gunsmith?"

She thought a moment, then said, "I suppose. I didn't realize . . ."

"Jesus," he said, "if I have the Gunsmith in my town I have to know."

He started to turn back, then stopped and stared at Rosemary.

"Go ahead," she said. "I can find a hotel by myself."

"Just got a couple of more blocks," he said. "The hotel's on the left. It's very reasonable. Just don't go near the Big Rock Hotel. That's the expensive one."

"I understand."

"Jesus," he said, "the Gunsmith," and rushed back the way they had come.

SIX

The sheriff entered the doctor's office again, heard voices in the other room. He stuck his head in and saw the doctor standing over a prone Clint Adams.

"Hey, Doc Jacobs?"

The doctor turned. "I'll be there in a minute, Sheriff," Jacobs said. "Just need to finish up."

"Okay."

The sheriff sat by the doctor's desk, nervously bouncing his legs. When Jacobs entered, he jumped up.

"Doc, do you know who that is?"

"I do," the doctor said. "I assume this means that you do, too?"

"I had to make sure," Evans said. "Is it . . . him?"

"Is it who?"

"The Gunsmith!"

"Yes, it is."

"Jesus," Evans said, "the Gunsmith in my town. If word gets out, there'll be blood in the streets."

"You're bein' too dramatic, Cal."

"Am I? What do you think would happen if him being here became common knowledge?"

"I don't know."

"Gunmen will come out of the woodwork," Evans said, "that's what. How long is he stayin'?"

"I don't know."

"Well, how bad is he hurt?"

"I don't want to feed into your drama," Jacobs said.

"What do you mean?"

"At the moment," Doc Jacobs said, "the Gunsmith can't move his hand."

Evans stared at Jacobs.

"Sheriff?"

"Huh? Oh, uh, you mean . . . his gun hand?"

"That's what I mean," Evans said. "The puncture wound in his arm has affected the motor functions of his hand."

"Doc!"

"Like I said," Evans replied, "he can't use his right hand."

"Jesus!" Evans said. "If this got out, we'd be *drowning* in gunnies."

"Why would it get out?" the doctor said. "I'm not going to tell anyone. Are you?"

Clint stared down at his bandaged arm. The doctor had cleaned the wound as best he could and then stitched it closed. While the pain had subsided somewhat, Clint was very concerned that he could not move his hand.

His gun hand.

The one that had kept him alive all these years.

He reached out to touch his gun belt, which was on a table within reach. He had fired his gun left-handed before, and was probably better than most. But that wouldn't help him against experienced guns. If he couldn't use his right hand, he'd be a sitting duck for every two-bit gunny who came along.

The doctor kept avoiding the subject of how long the paralysis would last, which made Clint worry that the man either didn't know—or he knew and wasn't telling.

He pushed himself to a seated position, swung his legs around so that his feet touched the floor. He was about to try to stand when he got dizzy. Spots appeared in front of his eyes, so he closed them and began to breathe deeply.

It didn't help. If the doctor hadn't come back in at that moment and caught him, the Gunsmith would have hit the floor.

SEVEN

When Clint came to, he was looking at the ceiling again.

"Doc?"

The doctor rushed in from the other room and looked down at him.

"How are you feelin'?"

"Terrible," he said. "Come on, Doc, you've got to tell me. How long is my hand going to be like this?"

"The truth is, I don't know, Mr. Adams," Doc Jacobs said. "There was significant damage to the ligaments in your arm."

"Will they heal?"

"That's what we have to wait to find out."

"How long?"

"Honestly? I have no idea."

"Doc, look," Clint said, "do you know who I am?"

"You're the second person to ask me that today. Yes, I do know who you are, Mr. Adams: the Gunsmith."

"If word got out that I couldn't use my right hand—" Clint started.

"I understand that, Mr. Adams. I assure you, no one is going to hear it from me."

"Second," Clint said.

"What?"

"You said I was the second person today to ask you that," Clint said. "Who was the first?"

"Oh, the sheriff. He just asked me that a little while ago."

"And what did you tell him?"

"What I told you."

"So he knows I can't use my right hand?"

"He does," the doctor said, "but as far as I know, he doesn't plan to tell anyone."

"But that doesn't mean he won't, at some point."

"He's the law, Mr. Adams."

"Sorry, Doc," Clint said, "but I've run into a lot of badge-toters who had their own ideas about upholding the law."

"I see."

"Can I leave?"

"You can't even stand," the doctor said.

"I can at least try that again."

"Okay," Jacobs said, "let's try it."

He helped Clint into a seated position, then backed away so the man could try to stand on his own. This time, Clint made it to his feet.

"Okay," he said. "I can stand."

"Next," the doctor said, "try takin' a step."

* * *

Rosemary got two rooms at the hotel. She figured she would share one with Jenny. The other three girls would share the second room. If Delilah and Morgan didn't kill Abigail by morning, it would be a miracle. Maybe Rosemary would take the older woman instead.

She waited in the lobby for the four other women to appear. They had brought whatever they could carry with them.

"How'd you know which hotel I'd be at?" she asked.

"We asked the man at the livery stable which hotel was the cheapest," Jenny said.

"Okay, here," she said, handing Jenny a key. "You share a room with Delilah and Morgan. Abigail, you're with me."

"Fine."

"Take our belongings to the rooms," she told them.

"Where are you going?" Abigail asked.

"I'm going to go and check on Clint."

"Why are you worried about that man?" Abigail asked. "We don't need him anymore."

"Abigail," Rosemary said, "he got hurt trying to help us."

"It wasn't our fault," Abigail said.

"It was *your* fault," Jenny said to her.

"It was not!"

"Yeah, it was," Morgan said.

"Girls," Rosemary said, "just go to your rooms. I'll be back in a while and then we'll get something to eat."

She turned and left them in the lobby, still arguing.

Clint took a step, then two, then three. There was no dizziness.

"I can walk," he said.

"But walking isn't the problem, is it?" the doctor asked.

"No," Clint said, "staying alive is."

"Until your arm heals and you can use your hand again," Jacobs said.

"Right."

Clint knew they were both thinking the same thing.

If his arm healed.

EIGHT

Rosemary entered the doctor's office and called out, "Hello?"

"In here," the doctor's voice answered in return.

She moved across the office into the examination room.

"What's going on?" she asked.

"I'm tryin' to convince your friend, Mr. Adams, that he needs to stay still a while longer."

"And Mr. Adams wants to go and get a hotel room and sleep in a real bed," Clint said.

"How is your arm?"

"Doesn't hurt as much," he said. "Apparently, the doctor says you kept me from bleeding to death. I'm much obliged."

"It was the least we could do," she said. "After all, you got hurt trying to help us."

"I guess the wheel made it, huh?" Clint asked.

"Luckily."

"Well, now you can get it fixed properly," Clint said.

She noticed that while Clint had his gun belt on, he wasn't really moving his right arm that much. She assumed it hurt him more than he was saying.

"What do I owe you, Doc?"

"I'll send a bill to your hotel."

"I don't know which one I'll be in."

"Is money a problem?"

"Not usually."

"Then you want the Big Rock Hotel. Best place in town."

"Might as well be comfortable while I'm recuperating, huh?" Clint asked.

"I'll stop in on you and see how you're doin'," Doc Jacobs said. "If I was you, I'd plan on being here for a few days, at least."

"Okay, Doc. Thanks."

"I can walk over with you, if you like," Rosemary said.

"That's a good idea," Jacobs said. "A pretty nurse can do wonders."

"Fine," Clint said. "She can catch me if I keel over again."

"Again?" she said, looking at the doctor.

"Just some residual dizziness from the loss of blood," Jacobs explained. "Don't let him get on a horse anytime soon. If he faints and falls off, he could do himself a lot of harm."

"I'll keep reminding him," Rosemary said.

Clint thanked the doctor again and walked out with Rosemary.

* * *

"We got the wagon to the livery. Your horse, too," Rosemary said.

"Thanks for that. I'll check in on him later."

"I think it's you who needs checking in on, Clint."

"As long as it's you, I won't mind," he said. "Just don't send Abigail."

"She doesn't like you."

"The feeling is mutual."

When they reached the hotel, he checked in, writing his name with his left hand, trying to look as if he'd been doing it all his life.

"Where are you all staying?" he asked.

"The other, less expensive hotel," she said. "We're on a budget."

"Why don't you let me take you out for a steak?" he asked.

"I really should eat with the other girls."

"Well, I'd take them, too, but—"

"You don't want them to see that you can't cut your meat?" she asked. "How about if I get two steak dinners and bring them to your room?"

"If they won't miss you too much."

"They're too busy fighting to notice I'm gone," she said. "You go to your room and I'll go get the food."

"Okay," he said. "Here." He passed her some money. "Splurge. Get the best."

"Okay. I'll be right back."

Clint made it to his room and sat on the bed. He wanted to get his boots off, but he needed both hands for that. Awkwardly, he unbuckled his gun belt and hung it on the bed-post.

He sat there, feeling helpless. When his left arm itched, he tried to scratch it, but he couldn't reach it. Helpless.

Until Rosemary came back.

He'd left the door unlocked. In just a little while, she walked in with a napkin-covered tray. The smell of meat was strong.

"Ready to eat?" she asked.

"I am," he said, "if you can help me off with my boots, first."

NINE

She cut up his steak and they ate with their plates on the bed, seated on the floor. She had taken him at his word and splurged. There were potatoes, onions, carrots, and rolls. And she'd carried a bottle of whiskey under her arm the whole way without dropping it. He would have preferred beer, but the whiskey would do.

She had helped him off with his boots, and then helped him change into a clean shirt.

"Where are you and the other women headed?" he asked.

"California."

"Husbands waiting there?"

"No husbands," she said. "Not for any of us."

"Well, you don't know that."

"Oh, future husbands," she said. "Well, then the answer is . . . maybe. But probably not for Abigail."

"Too old?"

"She hates men too much," she said.

"And the others?"

"They're all young," Rosemary said. "They look forward to the future."

"And you?"

"Not as young as them," she said, "but certainly not as old as Abigail."

"You got my boots off like a pro," he said. "You'd make a man a fine wife."

"I used to help my father off with his boots," she said. "Until he died."

"When was that?"

"A couple of years ago. He was the last family I had, so I decided to come west."

"How did you hook up with the others?"

"That happened one by one," she said. "They all have their reasons."

"What are they?"

"I'm afraid it's not up to me to reveal them," she said.

"Do you know?"

"Well . . . not all of them," she said. "I knew Delilah before this trip, but the others . . . well, we met just before we left."

"How did you meet?"

"I advertised for companions for this trip," she explained.

"Advertised?"

"In the St. Louis newspaper," she said. "I wanted to make the trip, but not alone."

"Did any men respond to the advertisement?" he asked.

"Yes," she said, "but I was only interested in traveling with women."

"Having a man along might have come in handy once or twice," he said. "Like today."

"God," she said, "was that only today? This morning?"

"I know," Clint said, "it seems much longer."

"It's been a long day for all of us," she said. She stood up and started picking up the plates. "I've got to bring these back to the cafe." She pointed to the whiskey bottle, still three-quarters full. "I'll leave that with you."

He stood up.

"I could use some coffee before I turn in," he said. "That cafe serve any?"

"I think I smelled some when I went in," she said.

"Good," he said. "I'll walk back with you."

He rolled down the sleeves on his shirt, making sure to button them so that the bandage on his gun arm couldn't be seen.

That done, he awkwardly strapped on his gun belt. Instinctively, she knew better than to offer to help with that.

Rosemary returned the plates and utensils to the waiter, and then she and Clint sat down and had some good coffee. At least, he thought it was good.

"Whoa," she said, "that's strong."

"That's the way coffee's supposed to be," he said, sitting with his right arm on the table. He was trying to make it seem natural, but was certain people were staring at him.

"It's all right," she told him.

"What is?"

"Your arm," she said. "Nobody notices."

"What are you, a mind reader?"

"Well, a man like you, with your reputation, you'd have to be worried somebody will notice."

"You're right," Clint said. "I probably should have stayed in the room."

"No," she said. "You have to seem normal, and then nobody will notice anything."

During the walk to the café Clint had been thinking he needed to buy a left-handed rig, just until his right arm healed. Now he was having second thoughts. A left-handed holster would tell people something was wrong with his right arm. But if somebody did make a try at him, he'd never be able to get the gun out left-handed in time. Not reaching across his body. Unless he reversed the gun in the holster, wore it butt forward. That'd make it easier to grab left-handed. Maybe nobody would notice if the gun sat butt-forward in his holster.

"What are you thinking?" she asked.

"Just that you're probably right," he said. "I need to look as natural as possible."

"How many people know you're not left-handed?" she asked.

"Probably people who know me," Clint said.

"There's nothing in your reputation about being right-handed?"

"I don't believe so."

"Then it's only folks who know you that'll notice something like you drinking coffee with your left hand," she said.

"I suppose that's right."

"Well then, just relax and enjoy your coffee," she said. "Maybe you'll feel better after a good night's sleep."

He found the sight and sound of her relaxing, so he decided to do what she said.

After coffee, Clint offered to walk Rosemary back to her hotel, since it was now dark.

"Maybe I should walk you," she said.

"Didn't we just finish talking about how everything needs to seem natural?" he asked. "That means I walk you back."

"Okay."

His money was in his right pocket, so he couldn't get to it with his left. In the morning he'd have to switch it. For now, Rosemary paid for the coffee.

They left the café and he walked her to her hotel.

"You can get your wagon fixed in the morning and be on your way," he said.

"I think we'll take a day or two here, get some rest before continuing on," she said. "Can I look in on you in the morning?"

"Sure," he said. "I'd like that. Goodnight, Rosemary."

"Goodnight, Clint."

He waited until she went inside, then walked back to his own hotel.

TEN

Clint woke in the morning lying on his back. He didn't move. If he stayed still for a while, there was a chance his right arm *would* move when he decided to try it. But until he tried, everything was okay.

He moved his left first, ran it over his face, dug a thumb and forefinger into his eyes to clean them out. Then he took a deep breath and tried to move his right arm. He was able to move it, and that was encouraging, but then he tried to move his fingers.

Nothing. A little pain, but they didn't move.

"Crap," he said. "Goddamnit!"

He sat up in bed, dragging his right arm with him. He got up, poured some water in a bowl from a pitcher and, one-handed, washed as well as he could.

He managed to get himself dressed, and then came to his boots. It had been a bitch getting them off the night before, but he'd finally done it. Getting them on one-handed was easier. All he had to do was get his foot in, and then stand up. When that was done, he strapped on his gun then turned the gun butt forward. He reached across his body a few times to grab it and managed to do so without dropping it.

He'd never gone to the livery the day before to check on Eclipse, so he decided that was the first thing he'd do, even before breakfast.

He left the room.

The sheriff woke in one of his cells. He spent a lot of nights there, because there was nothing waiting for him at home. He lived alone; what was the point of going there? When he went there he took the badge off, and when he took the badge off, he was nobody.

So he slept in one of his cells, and kept the badge on. He'd only stabbed himself in the chest with it a couple of times.

He went into his office and put on a pot of coffee. He had slept well, and was feeling good this morning. He had Clint Adams in his town. That was enough to perk anybody up. Clint Adams was a famous man, and trouble followed men like that. Cal Evans had been sheriff of Big Rock for five years, and in all that time nothing exciting had happened.

Until now.

He poured himself a cup of coffee. After he was finished, he'd go over and see how Clint Adams was doing. If word got out that the Gunsmith couldn't move his right arm, there would suddenly be a lot of excitement in this town.

A lot of it.

* * *

When Clint walked out the front door of the hotel, he did so with some trepidation. He stopped just outside, took a deep breath and looked around. No gunmen waiting for him to come out. That was encouraging.

But there was a man walking toward him, and he was wearing a badge.

"Mr. Adams," the sheriff said. "Nice to see you up and about."

"Have we met?" Clint asked.

"Briefly, yesterday," the lawman said. "I helped the ladies get you into the doctor's office."

"Much obliged, then, Sheriff."

"Where are you off to?"

"Wanted to go over to the livery and check on my horse," Clint said. "Maybe even see if the lady's wagon was being fixed."

"Mind if I walk with you?"

"Not at all."

They started to walk.

"I notice you're wearing your gun with the butt forward for a cross draw."

"I had hoped it wasn't that noticeable."

"Well, the doctor told me about your situation," the sheriff said. "No better today?"

"I'm afraid not."

"That's got to be a concern for a man like you," the sheriff said.

"It is."

"Can you shoot left-handed?"

"Very well," Clint said.

"That's good, but I don't expect there'll be any trouble. Not in this town," the sheriff said. "Hasn't been any for five years."

"That's good to hear."

They got to the livery and stopped in front.

"Fella named Leroy should be takin' care of your horse," he said. "He's good with animals."

"That's good."

"My name's Cal Evans, Mr. Adams," the lawman said. "You need anythin' while you're in town, you just let me know."

"I'm much obliged, Sheriff," Clint said, "but all I need is for word about my arm not to get around."

"You can count on me, Mr. Adams."

ELEVEN

Clint entered the livery and introduced himself to Leroy, a big black man of indeterminable age with a very easygoing manner.

"Dat big black horse is yours?" he asked. "Dat's one fine horse."

"Yes, he is," Clint said. "The sheriff assured me that you'd be taking good care of him. I just haven't seen him since yesterday."

"I understand," Leroy said. "A horse like that is special. He's in the back stall."

"Oh, and that wagon the ladies brought in yesterday?" Clint asked.

"I put a new carter key on it," Leroy said. "Good as new."

"You bill my horse and the repair on the wagon to me," Clint said.

"Whatever you say, mister."

"Thanks."

Clint walked to the back stall, found Eclipse standing comfortably. He looked as if he was freshly brushed, and he had plenty of feed.

"You haven't even missed me, have you, big boy?" Clint asked, stroking the horse's massive neck.

Eclipse nodded his big head emphatically.

"Yeah, okay," Clint said, "you're okay. I just had to make sure."

He left the stall, exchanged nods with Leroy, and left the livery.

Sheriff Evans left Clint at the livery and walked back to the center of town. Having Clint Adams in town was exciting, but if all he did was recover from his injury, it wouldn't do anything for the town, or for the sheriff. Evans had to figure out some way to make Clint Adams's presence work for him.

Clint went back to his hotel and into the dining room. He ordered a breakfast that would be easy for him to eat with one hand—a stack of flapjacks. While he was eating, Doc Jacobs came in and approached his table.

"Mind if I sit?" he asked.

"Hey, Doc," Clint said. "Have a cup of coffee."

"Don't mind if I do," he said. "I've been up all night with Mrs. Francis. Finally delivered twins."

"I admire you for being able to bring new life into the world, Doc."

"Wasn't me," the sawbones said. "It was her. I just helped."

"Yeah, well, without your help I'm sure it would've been a lot harder."

"Yeah, maybe." The doctor drank some coffee. "How are you feelin'?"

"Well, except for not being able to move any of the fingers on my right hand, I'm fine."

"You look okay," Jacobs said. "When I walked in, I never would have known you were injured."

"That's good."

"But if you have to go for your gun—"

"I decided not to advertise by wearing a left-handed rig, so if I need to, I'll cross draw."

"Will that be enough?"

"In most cases, yes," Clint said. "Unless I'm facing an experienced gun."

"Then what?"

"Then I'm dead."

"You say that calmly."

"Oh, there's nothing calm about dying," Clint said, "but it's going to happen sooner or later."

"Well, yes, death is unavoidable but how we die is sort of up to each one of us, isn't it?"

"Not me," Clint said. "I see my death happening one way. The same way Bill Hickok died, Ben Thompson died, and Jesse James died."

"They were all shot to death."

"Exactly. But I don't expect it to happen anytime soon. At least, not until my arm heals. When the time comes, I want to face it as a whole man. Then I can accept whatever happens. But this way . . ." Clint shook his head.

Jacobs poured himself some more coffee. "Well, like I said, no one's going to find out anything from me."

"I appreciate that, Doc."

Jacobs drained a second cup of coffee while Clint finished his flapjacks.

"Let's go to your room so I can examine you," Jacobs said. "Then I'm gonna get some sleep."

"Okay, Doc."

In Clint's room, the doctor took hold of his hand and manipulated each finger in turn.

"How's that feel?" he asked with each one.

"Hurts," Clint said each time.

The doctor lowered Clint's arm.

"What's that mean, Doc?"

"Well," he said, "you've got feeling. That's a lot better than if your arm and hand were completely numb."

"I guess."

The doctor undid Clint's sleeve and rolled it up. He removed the bandages so he could examine the stitches on the wound, then wrapped it anew.

Clint rolled the sleeve down and clumsily buttoned it.

"How would you feel about staying indoors until there's some change?" the doctor asked.

"That would attract attention," Clint said. "The word would go out that the Gunsmith was holed up in a hotel in Big Rock, Arizona. That would bring gunnies from all over the country, and they'd stand in line for a chance to kill me."

"I suppose you know your world best," the doctor said. "What about sending for help?"

"If I sent such a telegram, word would get out," Clint said.

"But you have friends who would help, I'm sure," the doctor said.

Clint thought about Bat Masterson and Wyatt Earp, who would always have his back. Also Luke Short, Neil Brown, Heck Thomas, Jim West . . . there were a handful of men he knew could watch his back. But he was used to helping himself, even in a position like this.

Well, actually, he'd never been in this position before. He'd always been able to count on his gun arm to get him out of any jam.

Only this time, his gun arm was useless.

"I'll have to think about it," he said. "A message like that would have to be sent in such a way that it couldn't be intercepted."

"That means you'd have to send it with someone you trust."

"And I don't see anyone in town who fits that description."

"What about one of the ladies?"

"I just met them yesterday, Doc," Clint said. "And they're women, not gunmen. I'd never put them in that kind of danger."

"Well," the doctor said, standing up and closing his big black bag, "it certainly sounds like you're describing a situation where you're entirely on your own."

"Sure looks that way, Doc."

TWELVE

After the doctor left, Clint paced his room, replaying the doctor's suggestion. Stay in this room until there was some change? What if that didn't happen? What if he never got the use of his right hand back?

Well, he could stay in the room and practice his cross draw, and venture out only when he was sure he could defend himself. But how long would that take? Word would still get out that he was holed up in a hotel room following an injury. What would gunmen assume from that? They'd correctly assume that something was wrong.

He had to go out.

As he made that decision, there was a knock at the door. He drew his gun with his left hand and opened the door.

"Good morning," Rosemary said. "Can I come in?"

"Actually," he said, sliding the gun back into the holster, "I was just coming out."

"Um, do you think that's wise?" she asked.

"I was already out," he said. "I went to see my horse, and to check on your wagon."

"Oh? And how is the wagon?"

He stepped out into the hall and closed the door behind him. "Your wagon is ready to go. You can ride out of town at any time."

"I think I'd like to stay a while," she said.

"And what about the others?"

"Oh, they're pretty much been looking at me as the leader since we left St. Louis," she said.

"And where are the rest of the ladies now?"

"Having breakfast somewhere."

"What about your breakfast?"

"Well, I thought I might have that with you, but since you were up early . . ."

"I could have some more coffee," he said. "The dining room here has a very good breakfast."

"Well, since I wasn't around to cut your meat for you, I'd guess you had something you'd be able to cut with your left hand. Flapjacks? Or something you didn't have to cut? Oatmeal?"

"Flapjacks."

"Would you mind if I had steak and eggs?"

"Not at all," he said. "It would be my pleasure to watch you cut your meat."

"Okay, then," she said, and they went into the dining room.

"She's with him," Abigail said. "I know it."

"What does it matter?" Morgan asked.

"She's supposed to be one of us," Abigail complained.

"She *is* one of us, Abigail," Jenny said.

Abigail, Jenny, Morgan, and Delilah were sitting in a café near their hotel, having breakfast. Only Abigail was complaining that Rosemary wasn't there with them, but then Abigail was always complaining about something.

"Then why isn't she here?" she asked.

"Abigail," Jenny asked, "Why doesn't anyone ever call you Abby?"

Abigail turned her head and looked at the other woman.

"What?"

"Yeah," Morgan said, "has anyone ever called you Abby?"

"No," Abigail said. "My name is Abigail, not Abby. I hate Abby. Don't call me Abby."

"Okay," Delilah said, "we won't call you Abby."

"In fact," Morgan said, "we won't ever say the word *Abby*. Right girls?"

"Right," Jenny said. "No Abby."

"I see what you're doing," Abigail said. "You're trying to get me off the subject. None of you care that Rosemary has set her cap for this man?"

"'Set her cap'?" Jenny asked. "Isn't that kind of old-fashioned?"

"Only to someone as young as you, Jenny," Abigail said. "The fact is, we're not in this town to look for husbands."

"Come on, Abigail," Delilah said. "We all left St. Louis to come west to look for husbands."

The other girls all laughed.

"Well, I did not!" Abigail said. "If that's truly the reason you all have made this trip, then I was recruited under false pretenses."

"Oh, come off it, Abigail," Morgan said. "We all came on this trek for our own reasons. And there's no reason we need to reveal them."

"You mean . . . you aren't all looking for husbands?" Abigail asked.

"No," Morgan said, looking at the other girls. "Well, I'm not."

"I want more biscuits," Jenny said.

Rosemary finished the last chunk of steak on her plate and put her fork down.

"How was it?" he asked.

"It was wonderful," she said. "Oh, I'm sorry. I should have offered you at least a bite."

"No, no," he said. "I enjoyed watching you enjoy it."

"I just seem to have such a big appetite since we came west," she said. "Is it the air?"

"It probably is," he said. "Fresh air does increase the appetite. When I'm on the trail, everything I eat tastes so good."

"Even beans?"

"Yes," he said, "even beans."

She sat back, put both hands over her belly, and said, "I hope I don't get fat."

"I can't imagine you fat," he said, "but even if you were, you'd be beautiful."

"Really?"

"Yes, really."

"Thank you, Clint."

"Now," he said, "if we take a walk, you'll work some of that breakfast off."

THIRTEEN

They walked around Big Rock, which didn't take very long. It was a town that seemed to have found its size. There was no sign of any sort of expansion.

"This looks like a nice, quiet place to live," Rosemary said. "I've seen a church, a playhouse, several shops for women, like a hat shop, dress shop—"

"—saloons," he said, "don't forget the saloons. And where there are saloons, there are men who drink too much. And I'm sure there's a whorehouse around here, someplace."

"Oh," she said. "Really?"

"That's every town in the West, Rosemary," he said. "They can all be nice places to live, but you also have to be aware of everything."

"I see."

"I just don't want you to think you've found any kind of paradise," he said.

"But I understood that the West had become somewhat . . . civilized?"

"Civilized, yes," Clint said. "Tame, no."

"I understand."

"Why did you decide to come out West, Rosemary?" he asked. "Do you mind if I ask?"

"We all had our own reasons," she said. "We haven't really shared them all."

"Well then," he said, "you don't have to tell me, either."

"Maybe," she said, "maybe later."

"Okay," he said. "Maybe later."

"I think I should go and find the others now," she said. "They were going to a café near the hotel."

"I'll walk with you," he said. "I'd like to say hello to them, and thank them for their help in getting me to the doctor."

"Oh, okay," she said. "Let's go."

None of the women noticed the two men who entered the café as they were finishing up their breakfast.

Zack Moody and Dan Rhodes had just come off the trail the day before. They'd had whiskey and steaks the night before, and then fallen into their beds in their hotel room.

Today they were looking for women. They thought they'd have breakfast first and then find some whores, but when they walked in and saw a tableful of women, they jumped to a conclusion.

"Hey Zack," Moody said. "Look. A tableful of whores, just waitin' for us."

"Well, lookee there," Zack said. "Let's go set with the gals, Moody."

The two men walked over to the girls, grabbed chairs from a nearby table, and sat down . . .

When Clint and Rosemary entered the café, Clint could sense the tension and fear in the air. There were several other diners in the place, but most of the apprehension was coming from a table with two men and five women seated at it.

"Come on in, friends," one of the men said. "We're havin' a party. Me and my buddy are tryin' to decide which whore we want."

"But he's got his own, Zack," Moody said. "He brought his own in—and she's tasty."

"Yeah," Zack said, "but I want this one." He put his hand on Jenny's arm and she shrank away.

"Get your hand off of her!" Abigail shouted and swatted his hand away.

"That one's got spirit, Zack," Moody said. "Too bad she's so old and ugly."

"You know," Zack said, "sometimes the old, ugly ones are the best in bed."

"Yeah, well you try her. I want this one," Moody said, pointing to Rosemary. He stood up. "You done with her, friend?"

"You've made a mistake, friend," Clint said. "None of these women are prostitutes."

"That right?" Moody asked. "Well, my friend Zack here, who's a few years older than me, tells me all women are whores. Is that right, Zack?"

"That's right, Moody," Zack said. "Every fuckin' one of them."

"Rosemary," Clint said, "take the ladies and go outside."

"Come on, girls."

They started to stand, but Zack reached out and grabbed Jenny's arm.

"Uh-uh," he said. "Not this one. I want her."

Jenny looked at Clint imploringly.

"Rosemary," he said, "take the others out."

"She ain't leavin', either," Moody said, pointing to Rosemary. "I want her!"

Rosemary said, "Abigail, take Delilah and Morgan and go outside. Now!"

The three women stood warily, as if they weren't sure the two men would let them leave.

"The rest of you people," Clint said to the other diners, "you better also get out."

They didn't waste any time. Three men and two women ran from the place. Including the waiter.

"Well," Zack said, "that just leaves us two, our whores . . . and you. You're extra weight, friend. You better leave."

"These women are leaving now," Clint said, "or you two aren't leaving at all. Your choice."

"Oh wait," Zack said. "I get it, Moody. He's their pimp."

"Oh, yeah," Moody said. "Well, pimp, don't worry. When we're done, we'll pay 'em, and you'll get your cut."

"He's not a pimp," Rosemary said, "and we are not whores."

"Really?" Zack asked. "Who is he, then?"

"His name is Clint Adams!" Jenny blurted, and then she put her free hand to her mouth.

The two men exchanged a glance.

FOURTEEN

Clint could see that the two men recognized the name. In fact, the one named Zack, who had been seated until that point, released Jenny's arm and stood up.

"Rosemary," he said, "take Jenny out."

"Come on, Jenny," Rosemary said, extending her hand to the younger woman, who grabbed for it anxiously. Rosemary pulled Jenny away from the table and pushed her out the door. However, instead of leaving, Rosemary remained standing in the doorway, half in and half out, so she could watch.

"What the hell is the Gunsmith doin' on this one-horse town?" Moody asked.

"What does that matter?" Clint asked. "The fact is, I am here, and I don't like seeing ladies treated as whores. Especially when the ladies are friends of mine."

He was going to leave the play up to the two men. He preferred not to cross draw on them if he didn't have to. He was also hoping they didn't notice that he was wearing his gun butt forward. This was one time he was hoping his reputation would work for him, and keep them from doing something stupid.

"How you want to play this, Zack?" Moody asked. "You want a shot at the Gunsmith?"

"What? Me, alone? No way."

"I mean the two of us," Moody said, keeping his eyes on Clint. "We can take 'im."

"That's the Gunsmith, Moody," Zack said. "Ain't none of them whores worth dyin' for."

"Listen to your friend, Moody," Clint said. "He's talking sense."

"I ain't gonna back down," Moody said.

"Zack?" Clint asked.

"Yeah?"

"You want out?"

Zack licked his lips, looked at his friend, then nodded jerkily and said, "Hell, yeah. I didn't mean—"

"Just get out," Clint said. "Don't talk."

Zack moved so fast he knocked over some chairs along the way. Rosemary moved out of his way before he could trample her.

"You damn coward!" Moody shouted.

"He's not a coward, Moody," Clint said. "He just wants to stay alive. Do you?"

Moody wet his lips and stared at Clint.

"Go ahead," Clint said. "Do it, or walk out, but let's get it over with."

Moody flexed the fingers of his gun hand, then slowly pulled it away from his holster.

"Okay, okay," he said. "I'm leavin'."

Clint kept a wary eye on the man as he made his way to the door. He exchanged a glare with Rosemary as he left. Clint moved to the door and stood next to her.

Outside, Moody had to walk past the other women, all of whom glared at him. Even from the back, Clint could see something in the man's demeanor change. Having to walk past the women with his tail between his legs didn't set right with him.

He turned and looked at Clint.

"I can't do it," he said. "I can't walk away."

"Rosemary," Clint said, "move away."

"No," she muttered. "He'll kill you."

"Maybe," he said. "Just do it."

She put some distance between herself and Clint.

"Whenever you're ready, Moody," Clint said.

The women scattered, but watched. From across the street, Zach was also observing.

Clint didn't know what the man was thinking. He was so slow when he went for his gun that Clint easily outdrew him, even left-handed. Clint fired once, the bullet punching Moody right in the chest. The man went down on his back in the street.

Clint returned his gun to its holster. Normally, he would have ejected the spent round and replaced it with a live one, but he would have had to do it one-handed, and that would have made his injury obvious.

No one had been watching except for the women, and Zach. But after the shot many more people appeared, anxious to be present if there was any more shooting.

Clint walked to the dead man, kicked the gun away, and bent over to check and make sure he was dead. He looked up as Zack approached.

"You, too?" he asked.

Zack raised his hands and said, "No, no, not me."

"He's your partner," Clint said. "You take care of him."

"Yes, sir."

Clint turned as Rosemary came up next to him.

"You did it!"

"Not now," he said, as he saw the sheriff pushing through the crowd. He went to meet him.

FIFTEEN

"You outdrew him left-handed?" the sheriff asked.

They were in his office, having finally dispersed of the crowd and gotten the body removed from the street.

"He was slow," Clint said. "I was lucky."

"You think anybody noticed that you drew with your left hand?"

"I don't know," Clint said. "I hope not."

"What about his partner?"

"I think he was too scared to notice."

"You better hope so," the lawman said. "What about the crowd?"

"They weren't there for the shooting," Clint said. "They came afterward."

"Well, I heard from three or four men who said they saw the shooting, that they never seen anybody faster than you."

"Then they're lying," Clint said. "First, nobody was

there, and second, I was slow. If Moody had any experience at all, I'd be dead."

"But the word goin' around town is you're as fast—or faster—than ever."

"That may be," Clint said, "but the word is also going around that I'm *in* town."

"That's not good."

"No, it's not."

"What are you gonna do?"

"The doc doesn't want me ridin' for a while," Clint explained. "The ladies are just about ready to leave in their wagon. I think I'll just go with them."

"Sounds like a good idea," the sheriff said. "Who would suspect the Gunsmith of traveling with five women?"

"No one, I hope," Clint said. "And I'd like to keep it that way. Only you and the doctor would know anything about it."

"Why tell the doctor?"

"I don't think he'd let me leave if he thought I was going to be riding."

"Well," Sheriff Evans said, "I'm sure as hell not gonna tell anyone."

"I appreciate that, Sheriff," Clint said. "Of course, if anyone did hear about it I'd have to figure it was either you or the doctor."

"Well . . . yeah . . ."

Clint went to the doctor's office to bounce the idea off of the sawbones.

"I don't see why not," the doctor said, "As long as you don't try to drive the team."

"Not me, Doc," Clint said, "I'll have five women to drive for me."

"Sounds good to me," the doctor said.

"If they'll have me."

"You haven't asked yet?"

"No."

"Well," the sawbones said, tying off Clint's new bandage, "good luck . . ."

"Thanks."

"Heard you had some excitement today."

"Some."

"Got lucky?"

"Very."

"It's good to have luck," Doc Jacobs said. "Just don't count too heavily on it."

"I never do, Doc," Clint said. "Believe me."

When Clint came out of the doctor's office, Rosemary was waiting for him.

"Are you all right?"

"I'm fine," he said. "I still can't move my right arm, but otherwise, I'm fine."

"But . . . you killed a man."

"Yes."

"How . . . does that make you feel?"

"Not good," he said.

"But does it bother you?"

"It used to, a lot," he said. "Now it bothers me depending on who the person was. Somebody like this man doesn't bother me very much."

"What are you going to do now?"

"Leave town before word gets out that I'm here," he said.

"But . . . can you ride?"

"No," he said, "but I was wondering if you ladies would give me a lift."

"To where?"

He shrugged. "To wherever."

She smiled. "It would be our pleasure, Clint."

SIXTEEN

Rosemary presented Clint's request to the other women.

"He wants to come with us?" Jenny asked.

"Yes."

"For how long?" Morgan asked.

"I don't know," Rosemary said. "Maybe until his arm heals."

"But . . . will it heal?" Jenny asked.

"He hopes so."

"He did fine with his left hand today," Delilah pointed out. "I'd feel safer having him along with us the rest of the way. Or part of the way."

"So you say yes?" Rosemary asked.

"Yes," Delilah said.

"Jenny?"

"Yes."

"Morgan?"

"Oh, yes."

They all looked at Abigail, knowing what she was going to say.

"Well, I say no," she said. "He's dangerous."

"Not to us," Rosemary said.

"Yes, to us. When the word gets out that he can't use his right arm, men will come after him. And we'll be in the middle."

"Who's going to pass the word?" Rosemary asked. "Aside from us, only the doctor and the sheriff know, and they're not going to tell anyone."

Abigail averted her eyes.

"Abigail," Rosemary pressed, "who's going to tell?"

Abigail didn't answer.

"Oh no," Rosemary said.

"What?" Jenny asked.

"She already told somebody," Morgan said.

"Abigail," Delilah said, "you didn't."

"It's not my fault!" Abigail wailed.

"That's what you said when Clint got hurt," Jenny said. "And you're the one who let the wagon fall on his arm."

"—I didn't. I . . ." Abigail stammered.

"Who could she have told?" Morgan asked. "We've been together . . . almost all the time."

"Almost?" Rosemary said. "Where did you go, Abigail?"

"I—I went to a store. I just wanted something . . . sweet," she said.

"You went out to buy candy and ended telling someone about Clint's arm?" Rosemary asked.

"A man came up to me and started talking to me," she said. "He seemed very interested in us."

"Us?" Rosemary asked.

"Well, eventually he asked about Clint."

"And you just had to tell him," Jenny said.

"I—I—before I knew what I was doing . . . yes."

"Damn it, Abigail!" Rosemary said.

"Are you trying to kill him?" Jenny asked. "First the wagon, and now this?"

"It's—it's not my fault!"

"I'll have to go and tell him our decision," Rosemary said, "but I'll also have to tell him what Abigail did."

"Maybe he won't come with us, then," Morgan said.

"That's up to him," Rosemary said, "but he deserves to know."

She walked to the door. They were in the room she was sharing with Abigail. "Don't let Abigail go anywhere!" she ordered before leaving.

Walking down the hall, she heard Abigail wail, "But it wasn't my fault!"

SEVENTEEN

Candy Nolan had beautiful skin, and lots of it. In fact, she had acres of flesh, all pale and smooth except for her pink nipples and pussy.

Big Paul Dillon lived up to his name. At six-foot-eight and 280 pounds, he always picked the biggest girl he could find in a whorehouse, and this one was no exception. As soon as he'd arrived in Denby, Arizona, he'd gone looking for the nearest whorehouse, and the largest whore. He'd found both.

He sat on the bed and watched her undress. When she was naked, she stood there for him to inspect. Her breasts were large and pendulous, her thighs large and powerful, her calves thick. But she was not sloppy fat. Her belly, though large, was firm. Dressed, a man might call her fat. Naked, she was simply a big girl.

"Okay?" she asked him.

"Okay."

"Now you, big boy."

He smiled, stood up, undid his trousers and dropped them. When his massive dick came into view Candy's eyes went wide.

"Oh, my!" she said. "I hit the jackpot."

She got on her knees in front of him and took him in both hands.

"Jesus, it's not even hard yet and I can't hold it in two hands."

Big Paul had already removed his boots. Now he discarded his shirt so that he stood naked in the center of the room.

Candy stroked his dick until it began to swell, then took it into her mouth. As she began to suck it, he closed his eyes. This whore was very good at what she did. It was going to be a good experience.

For both of them . . .

Downstairs, a man came into the whorehouse carrying a telegram.

"Lookin' for a girl, son?" the madam asked.

"No, I'm lookin' for Paul Dillon."

"He's upstairs."

The young man started up.

"No," the woman said, "you can't go up there. Not without a girl."

He looked into the sitting room, where a couple of less-than-desirable-looking whores were sitting, clearly bored.

"I'll wait," he decided.

Dillon breathed heavily as Candy slid his massive cock in and out of her mouth. She couldn't take all of him, but he was impressed by how much of it she managed to accommodate.

Finally, he couldn't take it anymore. He reached down, put his hand under her arms and lifted her up, off the floor and dumped her on the bed.

"Oh my!" she said happily. "No man has ever been able to manhandle me like that. Makes me feel like I weigh ninety pounds."

"If you weighed ninety pounds, you wouldn't be in this room with me."

He got on the bed with her, took her tits in his hands, and squeezed them. She reached down to take hold of his cock and stroke it. They were both happy with what they had.

He leaned down and took one hard nipple in his mouth, sucked it avidly, then moved on to the other one. They were the biggest, thickest nipples he'd ever had between his teeth.

At one point he realized he could smell her cunt. She was wet and ready. He got to his knees between her big thighs, grabbed her legs, and spread them.

"Come on, big boy," she said. "Do it."

He pressed the spongy head of his cock to her wet pussy, and slid it up and down a bit to wet it, causing her to groan and bite her lip. Then, suddenly, he slid his long dick into her and she gasped, lifted her powerful legs and wrapped them around him.

"Oooh," she groaned, "yes, fuck me, big man."

He did. He fucked her hard. So hard that it seemed that their combined weight might make the bed fall apart . . .

* * *

Downstairs, everyone could hear the bed jumping up and down, and waited for the ceiling to come down.

"Gotta be Candy and that big fella," the madam said to the girls.

"Dillon," the man with the telegram said. "Paul Dillon."

"Am I supposed to know that name?" she asked.

"No," the young man said, brandishing the telegram, "but you will."

EIGHTEEN

Rosemary walked across the street to Clint's hotel and knocked on his door. He answered, gun in hand.

"I've talked to the girls about you coming along," she said, "but there's something you should know."

"Come on in."

He holstered the gun and turned to face her.

"So they said no?" he asked.

"On the contrary," she said. "They all said yes . . . except Abigail."

"Does the vote have to be unanimous?"

"No," Rosemary said, "she was outvoted. But now it's up to you. You might not want to come along."

"Why not?"

"Abigail let it slip to some man in a shop today about your arm."

"Oh."

"Are you angry?"

"I should be, I suppose," he said. "But it was bound to get out."

"If you still want to ride with us, you're welcome—if you can do it without killing her."

"I'll do my best. Yes, of course I still want to come. It's better than staying here and waiting for some young gun to come along."

"When do you want to leave?"

"I'm a passenger," he said. "You tell me where and when and I'll be there."

"Why don't you let me cut your meat again tonight. I'll let you know then?"

"I'm pretty hungry," he said.

"Can we meet in an hour? I should know by then when everybody wants to leave."

"Okay," he said. "An hour."

She smiled and said, "I'll come here and get you."

"That's fine."

"Good."

He opened the door for her and watched her walk down the hall, then closed it.

Dillon rolled off of Candy and sat on the edge of the bed.

"Are we done?" she asked. "Already?"

"I only paid for an hour," he said.

"Oh." She pouted in disappointment. "Don't have any more money, then?"

He looked at her. Her dark hair was tousled, her lips swollen from kisses. There was a bite mark on her left tit, next to the nipple. And he could still smell her cunt, wanted to bury his face in it. Would have, too, if he hadn't become impatient to fuck her.

She noticed his penis swelling again, beginning to jut from his lap.

"Not for this, I don't," he said. "Sorry."

"I'm sorry, too," she said.

He stood up to get dressed, his dick wagging at her. She reached out and took it in her right hand.

"Tell you what," she said. "You tell me what hotel you're in and I'll come to your room tonight."

He frowned. "For free?"

She grinned sheepishly. "Unless you want me to pay you," she said.

"I've never heard of a whore givin' it away for free," he said suspiciously.

"Well, to tell the truth," she said, "I've never been with a man as large as you. I really enjoyed it. Usually, these skinny little men pick the skinny whores. I get the ones who smell, or are just curious. Whatever their reason for coming upstairs with me, they usually just climb aboard, rut, and roll off. You're different. I'd like to spend more time with you."

"Well, that's fine with me," he said. "I don't usually find women your size. I pick the biggest one, but they're still usually too small. They get kind of . . . scared when they see me."

She stroked his hard cock and said, "I can see why. Some of the little girls downstairs would worry that you'd kill them with this thing."

"I'm at the hotel just across the street."

"For how long?"

"At least tonight," he said. "I'm only passin' through."

"Too bad," she said. She slid her hand down to cup his heavily hanging balls. "But at least we'll have tonight."

"All night?" he asked.

"Oh, yes," she said. "All night long."

When Dillon came downstairs, he had a spring in his step.

"Happy?" the madam asked.

"Very."

"Good. There's a young man here waitin' for you in the parlor."

Dillon leaned over to look in and saw his young partner, Lou Raymond.

"Lou!" he called.

The young man was glad to get away from the two skinny, unattractive whores and rushed to Dillon.

"We got this—"

"Outside," Dillon said.

They both stepped outside, walked a few blocks away, and stopped.

"Okay."

"Telegram," Raymond said. "The madam wouldn't let me bring it upstairs. Not without a girl."

"Why didn't you pick one?" Dillon asked, taking the telegram.

"Did you see them? They both probably have diseases."

Dillon read the telegram, then read it again. "The Gunsmith," he said, "in Big Rock."

"And injured," Raymond said. "Real bad."

Dillon folded up the telegram and put it in his pocket.

"We headin' for Big Rock?" Raymond asked.

"We are," Dillon said, thinking about Candy, "in the morning."

NINETEEN

This time, Clint went to a restaurant with Rosemary. They sat in a corner and she cut his meat as discreetly as she could. They both ordered the same steak dinner, so she simply cut up the one in front of her, then traded plates with him.

"Well done," he said.

"I can be sneaky when I have to be."

They ate and talked about Abigail.

"She's bitter," she said. "Has been mistreated by men, and now she's . . . old."

"Not so old," Clint said. "She looks . . . fifty."

"To a woman, that's old," she said. "Especially an unmarried woman."

"An old maid?"

"She was married once before, so I don't think she can be called an old maid," she said. "But he was the first man to mistreat her."

"And what happened?"

"He was killed."

"By who?"

"Nobody knows," she said. "He had a job, was walking home from work one night, and was killed. It looked like he was robbed."

"Do you think Abigail did it?"

Rosemary hesitated. "I feel bad to say that sometimes I do wonder," she said, finally, "but I doubt it."

"How does she get along with the other girls?"

"Not well," Rosemary said. "Abigail is a complainer, and nothing is ever her fault."

"Like this?" he said, indicating his arm.

"Yes, exactly like that," Rosemary said. "All the girls blame her for your injury."

"I don't."

"You're a rare man, then."

"It sounds like Abigail is her own worst enemy," Clint said. "I wouldn't want to add to that. I was under that wagon willingly."

"Well," Rosemary said, "I'll see if I can get her to stop talking, but I doubt it."

"So when are we leaving?" he asked around a bite of steak.

"In the morning," she said. "I thought we'd all meet for breakfast and leave right after."

"What about supplies?"

"The girls shopped today," she said. "We'll be able to cook on the trail."

"Does somebody do the cooking?" Clint asked.

"We share it," she said. "At least, Morgan, Delilah, and I share it. Do you cook?"

"I'm a good trail cook," he said. "If I can do it left-handed, I make the best trail coffee."

"We may let you do that," she said. "None of us seem to be able to make a decent pot of coffee."

Clint made a mental note to be sure to be the one who made the coffee.

He walked her back to her hotel, but not back to her room. They stopped just in front.

"Why don't you all come to my hotel for breakfast?" he said. "We'll meet in the lobby."

"All right," she said. "Does that include Abigail?"

"Yes, Rosemary," he said, with a smile, "that includes Abigail."

The next morning, Clint met the five women in the lobby and took them into the dining room.

All of the women were animated, happy to get back on the trail, and even happier to have Clint Adams along.

Except, of course, Abigail.

She kept quiet, and was careful never to look at Clint.

He wondered if he should make some sort of overture to her, maybe tell her that he didn't blame her for anything, but he was afraid he knew what her reaction would be. She'd attack, claim she wasn't to blame, that she had nothing to be forgiven for, and would probably say she had her own reasons for not wanting him along.

He decided not to ruin a beautiful morning by getting into an argument with her. There would probably be plenty of those on the trail.

Instead, they ate breakfast. He bantered with the other

women and then paid the bill. They left and walked over to the livery together.

They'd had their supplies delivered and packed onto the wagon for them, and the liveryman had hitched up their team and saddled Clint's horse for him.

He thought about trying to ride Eclipse for a while, but the women wouldn't hear of it. They insisted he ride in the back. So Rosemary drove and Abigail sat up front with her; Jenny, Delilah, and Morgan rode in the back with Clint.

That was the way they left Big Rock.

TWENTY

Big Paul Dillon woke the next morning feeling pleasantly exhausted. He and the big whore, Candy, had fucked most of the night, and his legs felt like wet noodles.

He rolled over and looked at her. She was lying on her back, big breasts leaning to either side but still full and round. Her pink nipples were flat, and he was tempted to stick his tongue on them so they'd pucker and swell, but decided against it. If he got started with her, they'd be going at it again and he was supposed to meet Lou Raymond at the livery stable in about twenty minutes.

Hmm, he thought, twenty minutes.

He leaned over and licked one nipple, then the other. She came awake, along with her nipples . . .

"You're late," Raymond complained.

"I know it."

Raymond had already saddled both horses, so they climbed aboard.

"You was fuckin' your brains out all night, wasn't ya?" Raymond asked.

"You bet," Dillon said happily.

"With that fat whore?"

"She's not fat," Dillon said. "She's big."

"Big, fat, same thing."

Dillon gave Raymond a hard stare. "You sayin' I'm fat?"

"Hell, no, Paul," Raymond said quickly. "I didn't say that."

"It's a beautiful morning," Dillon said, "and I'm feelin' good. Why would you want to ruin that for me, Lou?"

"I d-don't, Paul, honest," Raymond said, wishing he'd kept his mouth shut.

"Then let's just ride, Lou," Dillon said. "Let's not argue."

"That suits me, Paul."

"'Cause if we argue, I might get mad," the big man said. "You don't want me to get mad, do you?"

"N-no, Paul," Lou Raymond said, "I—I sure don't want ya to get mad."

"Good," Dillon said. "Now lead out, and keep your mouth shut."

TWENTY-ONE

"How's your arm?" Jenny asked.

"Kind of sore," Clint said.

"We're bouncing around a lot," Morgan said. "Do you want me to ask Rosemary to take it easy?"

"No, that's okay," Clint said. "She's doing the best she can."

They had only been riding half a day. It was way too soon for Clint to start complaining, but the jostling was making his arm ache.

"Try this," Delilah said, handing him a pillow.

"Thanks," he said. He set his arm on the pillow and immediately felt some relief. "That helps."

The three girls had been fawning over him since they left town. Water, something to eat, did he want to put his feet up, did he want one of them to hold his arm?

The pillow was the first offer he'd taken, and it worked.

For a while, anyway . . .

* * *

Dillon and Raymond rode into Big Rock around midday. They reined in their horses in front of the Red Garter Saloon, only the sign was so worn out it read RE GART SAL.

They walked in, found the bartender and one other man in the place.

"You boys must be in the wrong place," the black bartender said. "Don't nobody drink in here, no more."

"No," the lone man at the bar said, "they ain't in the wrong place. Three beers, Anton."

"Comin' up."

Dillon put his hand out, shook with the other man.

"Quentin," he said, "this here's Lou Raymond, been ridin' with me about a year."

"You learn not to make him mad, yet?" Quentin asked.

"I learned," Raymond said.

"Yeah, the hard way, right?" Quentin asked with a wry grin. "Like to broke my jaw the first time."

"You fellas rode together?"

"A while back," Quentin said.

He and Dillon were in their thirties; Raymond was about ten years younger.

The bartender set three beers down on the bar. Dillon took a sip.

"It's warm."

"Guess that's why don't nobody drink here no more," Anton said.

Raymond drank down the beer, anyway. At least it was wet.

"Adams still here?" Dillon asked Quentin.

"Nope," Quentin said. "Rode out early today with a bunch of women."

"Women?"

"Well, he rode in with them," Quentin said. "Got hurt helpin' them fix their wheel. Rode out again today, his arm all bandaged up."

"Which arm?" Dillon asked.

"Right one."

"Gun arm."

Quentin nodded.

"How bad?" Dillon asked.

"The lady I talked to said he can't move it at all. The right hand, I mean."

"He ridin' his horse?"

Quentin shook his head.

"He's ridin' in the back of their wagon, his horse tied to the back."

"You saw this yourself?"

"Yup. Watched them ride out."

Dillon sipped his warm beer, made a face, and pushed it away. Raymond grabbed it and drank it.

"That it?" Dillon asked.

"No," Quentin said. "Adams killed a man while he was here."

"How?"

"Left-handed."

"Somebody drew on him?"

"Yeah."

"And he killed him, left-handed?"

"He must've," Quentin said, "because he can't use his right hand."

"Did you see him draw left-handed?"

"No. Nobody saw it."

"So then you can't be sure that he can't use his right hand."

"That's what the lady told me."

"Why'd she tell you that?"

"She likes to talk," Quentin said. "She has a big mouth."

"She tell you about her friends?"

"Yep," Quentin said. "She complained about them."

"Okay," Dillon said. "Come on."

"Where?"

"Someplace I can get a cold beer," Dillon said. "And you're gonna tell me about these women."

TWENTY-TWO

The wagon came to a stop. Rosemary stuck her head in the back of the wagon.

"We're going to camp here," she said. "It'll be dark in an hour."

If Clint had been on horseback, and darkness was an hour away, he would have kept riding, but Rosemary was in charge of this trek to California.

"We all have our jobs when we camp," Jenny said. "I have to collect wood."

"So do I," Morgan said.

"I have to see to the team," Delilah said, "with Abigail. She helps me unhitch them, and then I take care of them."

"Who cooks?" Clint asked.

"Rosemary will tonight," Jenny said.

"I'll make the coffee," Clint said.

"We'll help you out of the wagon," Jenny said.

"I think I can get out myself," Clint said.

The three women climbed out ahead of him, then stood

by while he got himself out. He knew if he fell they would have caught him.

Rosemary and Abigail had already gotten down, and Rosemary came walking over to him.

"How was the ride?" she asked.

"Bearable."

"I'm sorry it was so bumpy. I couldn't avoid—" she started.

"You don't have to apologize for the terrain, Rosemary," he said. "You did fine."

"Did the girls take care of you?" she said.

"They saw to my every need."

"How's the arm?"

"Kind of sore," he said, "but the girls gave me a pillow, and that helped."

"Good," she said, "I told them to take care of you."

"I'm making the coffee, right?" he reminded her.

"And I'm cooking," she said. "Let's go."

Jenny and Morgan collected the wood for the fire and got it started. They had a barrel affixed to each side of the wagon for water. Jenny went and got a whole potful to be used for coffee and cooking.

Clint was able to make the coffee one-handed, and then Rosemary started cooking.

"Bacon and beans," she said. "But I also have some peppers and onions to put in it, so it's not just plain trail food. It's better."

"I'll be the judge of that," he said, and gave her a smile.

By the time it was dark, they were sitting around the fire, eating.

* * *

Over cold beers, Quentin filled Dillon in on who the women were, and how many.

"Can they use guns?" he asked.

"She said one of them could shoot a rifle, but that was it."

"This lady told you a lot," Dillon said.

"I know," Quentin said, "I was surprised. She just kept talkin'."

Raymond came and sat down with another cold beer, his fourth. Dillon was still on his second, as was Quentin.

"Slow down, Lou," Dillon said. "You'll be useless in the whorehouse later."

"Don't you worry about me and whores," Raymond said. "I'll be just fine with them."

"Okay," Dillon said. "We'll see."

"You headin' out in the mornin'?" Quentin asked.

"Yep," Dillon said. "They can't be goin' very fast. We should be able to catch up to them tomorrow."

"You gonna take him on the road?" Quentin asked.

"I don't think so," Dillon said.

"When, then?"

"I think we'll follow them 'til they get to a town. I'll take him then."

"You want witnesses, right?" Quentin said.

"Oh yeah," Dillon said. "As many as I can get. When I outdraw and kill the Gunsmith, I want everybody to see."

"You still got that weird gun?"

"What's weird about my Peacemaker?" Dillon asked. He took it out and put it on the table. Because his hands were so large, and his fingers so big, he'd had the trigger replaced with a larger one. He'd had the butt extended, and the holster adjusted to accommodate those changes.

"Look at it," Quentin said, "I couldn't fire that accurately."

"That's good," Dillon said, putting the gun back in his holster. "Less chance my own gun can ever be used against me."

"Are we done here?" Raymond said. "I wanna get some food, and then a whore."

"I wanna ride with you tomorrow," Quentin said.

"Well," Dillon said, standing up, "come and eat with us and we'll talk about that."

TWENTY-THREE

Dillon went to the whorehouse with Raymond, and while his partner picked out a pretty little blonde who weighed barely ninety pounds—and looked "clean"—Dillon could not find a girl big enough for his needs. He'd been spoiled by Candy from Denby a couple of days ago. Instead, he left the whorehouse and went back to the saloon—the one with the cold beer.

Quentin wasn't there when he walked in, but Dillon had already agreed to let his old partner tag along.

"I just wanna see it," Quentin said. "I wanna see you gun the Gunsmith."

"I told you," Dillon said, "the more witnesses the better."

Dillon went to the bar and ordered a beer. In the mirror, he saw the batwings open, and a man walked in. When he turned to come to the bar, Dillon saw the badge. He didn't know the man, but he was well acquainted with what he stood for.

Sheriff Cal Evans stood at the bar a few spaces from Dillon and ordered a beer.

"Quiet town," Dillon said to Evans.

"Usually."

"Heard you had some excitement a few days ago," Dillon said.

"Heard that, did ya?" Evans asked. "What'd you hear, exactly?"

"Heard the Gunsmith was in town," Dillon said. "That he gunned a man."

"Well, yeah," Evans said, over his beer, "that's true."

"Heard he did it left-handed."

Evans stared at Dillon, sipping his beer.

"That I can't tell ya," the lawman said. "I didn't see it."

"Must've been a big crowd."

"Actually, no," Evans said. "It happened so fast, nobody in town saw it."

"I heard some women saw it."

"Well, yeah," Evans said, "but they were with Adams. And they all left town, after."

Well, that pretty much confirmed everything Dillon had heard so far. Now he needed to find out if the sheriff knew anything extra.

Clint poured coffee for everyone, and then held his cup while Rosemary filled it for him.

"Thank you," he said.

"Oh, my God," Jenny said. "That's strong coffee."

"Kills any germs that might get into your food," Clint said.

"What?" Morgan said. "What germs?"

"There are no germs in this food," Rosemary said aloud.

She handed out the plates. Clint set his plate on his lap and ate with his left hand. He was able to use his right arm, at least, to keep the plate from sliding off his lap.

He tasted Rosemary's beans and bacon and his eyebrows went up. "This is really good, Rosemary," he said.

"See?" she said. "Not just regular trail food."

"Suits me," Clint said.

They all ate avidly; the job of cleaning up fell to Jenny.

While she took the plates and utensils away to clean them, they all had some more coffee, and Clint put another pot on the fire.

Rosemary said, "I see you're moving your arm more. Do you have any feeling in your fingers?"

"No," he said. "Nothing so far."

"Will you see another doctor when we get to another town?"

"Maybe," he said. "I don't know what good it would do."

"Maybe another doctor would know more," she said.

"Maybe."

He sipped his coffee.

"Are you depressed, Clint?"

"Oh yeah."

"But you can't give up," she said. "Maybe if we did some exercises?"

"Like what?"

"We could all take turns massaging your hand, maybe moving the fingers around?"

"Well, it sounds pleasant," he said. "I'm sure Abigail won't be volunteering for a turn."

"That doesn't matter," she said. "The four of us will do it, if you like."

He looked down at his right hand, which was curled up in his lap. What harm could it do, he wondered?

"Why not?"

TWENTY-FOUR

"What makes you so interested in the Gunsmith?" Evans asked Dillon.

Dillon had asked a few questions designed to elicit information from the lawman, but Evans had resisted responding.

"Well, hey," Dillon said, "he's the Gunsmith, ain't he? And I just missed seein' him by what? A day? I'm just curious."

"Well, there ain't nothin' else to know," Evans said. He finished his beer and set the empty mug down on the bar. "I got rounds to make. You stayin' in town long?"

"Just overnight," Dillon said. "Leavin' in the mornin'."

"Well, enjoy the rest of your stay," the sheriff said.

"Yeah," Dillon said, "have a good night."

The big man watched in the mirror as the lawman left the saloon.

* * *

Sheriff Evans had not been able to figure out how to use the Gunsmith to his benefit when the man was in town. Now came this big fella with the odd-looking rig on his hip, asking questions about Clint Adams. So the word had probably gotten out that Adams was in Big Rock, and might be easy pickings.

Evans went back to his office, unsure of what to do. Should he send some telegrams ahead to towns Adams and the women might pass through, with a warning? Or should he get on a horse, ride after them, and alert them himself?

In the end, he decided his responsibility was to his town, not to Clint Adams. Big Rock had survived the presence of Clint Adams and remained a small, quiet town, and he was going to have to be satisfied with that.

If the big fella left town the next day and caught up to Clint Adams, it would be out of the jurisdiction of Sheriff Cal Evans. There was nothing he could do about it.

He wondered how the big man had heard about Adams. Who had let the word out?

Dillon decided to make one more stop in the morning before leaving town and tracking Adams. He didn't bother looking for Raymond or Quentin. Let them find him. He had breakfast in his hotel dining room, then headed for the doctor's office.

When the big man entered his office, Doc Jacobs looked him up and down. For a man his size, the sawbones thought he looked extraordinarily healthy.

"Can I help you, my friend?"

"I think so," Dillon said. "You had a patient a few days ago. Clint Adams? I'd like to know what his condition was when he came to you, and what it was when he left town."

"I don't discuss my patients with strangers," Jacobs said. "In fact, I don't discuss them with anyone, so I'm afraid I can't help you, after all."

"No," Dillon said, "I think you can. Or maybe I should say, I think you better."

"Now, see here—"

The big man closed on him with surprising speed and grabbed him by the throat with unsurprising strength. His powerful hand quickly cut off the doctor's air supply.

"Lemme explain somethin' to you, Doc," Dillon said. "You don't wanna make me mad. Bad things happen when I get mad. You understand?"

The doctor couldn't speak, so he nodded his head as best he could.

"Now I'm gonna let you go, and you're gonna answer my questions. Understand?"

He nodded again and the big man released the hold.

"Now, tell me about the injury to Clint Adams."

Doc Jacobs cleared his throat a few times before speaking. "A wagon came down on his right arm, puncturing it," he said. "I stitched and bandaged it."

"That it?"

"That's it."

"How bad was the injury?"

"It was a deep puncture."

"You're tiptoin' around, Doc," Dillon said. "I can feel myself gettin' mad again. How bad was the injury?"

"He could not use his right hand," the doc said.

"There you go," Dillon said. "How long is that condition gonna last?"

"There's no way of knowing."

"Could it be permanent?"

"There's no way of—it could be," the doc said as Dillon started to reach out for him.

"Could be?"

"It's . . . likely."

"There you are," Dillon said. "See, I ain't mad anymore."

"How could it benefit you to kill a one-armed man?" the doctor asked.

"It would benefit me to kill the Gunsmith if he had no hands," Dillon said. "The newspapers will say 'Dillon Outdraws the Gunsmith, or 'Dillon Kills Gunsmith.' They won't say how many arms he had, Doctor."

"So it's about reputation?"

"It's all about reputation, Doc," Dillon said. He turned to leave, then turned back. "If I find out you sent a telegram and warned Adams, I'll come back."

"If you're alive."

"I believe what you told me about Adams's arm," Dillon said. "Don't worry, I'll be alive."

Dillon left to go in search of his two partners. Time to hit the trail.

TWENTY-FIVE

The doctor waited until Dillon was gone fifteen minutes, then left his office and hurried to the jail. He was out of breath by the time he entered. Evans looked up in surprise.

"Who's chasin' you, Doc?"

"I did somethin' terrible," the Doc said, "because I am a coward."

"Settle down, Doc," Evans said. "Have a seat."

The lawman took a bottle of whiskey from his desk drawer, poured some into a coffee cup, and handed it to the doctor, who downed it.

"Now tell me what you did."

Evans listened intently while the doctor told him of the big man's visit.

"Well, Doc," he said, when the sawbones was done, "I met the man you're talkin' about, so I can't say I blame you."

"B-but, we've got to warn Adams."

"How do we do that?" Evans asked. "We don't know where he and those women went."

"Can't you figure it out?"

"I don't even know what direction they went when they left town."

Jacobs's shoulders slumped and he said, "What have I done?"

"Doc," Evans said, "Adams is gonna have to face this kind of situation sooner or later. If this man—"

"Dillon," Jacobs said. "He said his name was Dillon."

"If this man Dillon kills the Gunsmith, you can bet we'll hear about it."

"And if Adams kills him?"

"We won't hear a word," Evans said. "That's the way it is with reputation. No one notices the dead man who didn't have one."

"Ridiculous," Evans said. "Men are killed for the most ludicrous reasons."

"Maybe Adams can take this man left-handed, like he did here in town."

"Maybe . . ."

"And maybe by the time Dillon finds him, he'll be able to use his right hand again."

"I doubt it," Jacobs said. "Even if he does get the use of his hand back, it'll be months before he can draw a gun effectively."

"Then all Dillon has to do is catch up to him," Evans said. "Maybe he's a lousy tracker."

"Adams told me he expected to die from a bullet," Jacobs said. "That just might be a self-fulfilling prophecy."

Sheriff Evans wasn't sure what that was, but it didn't sound good.

Dillon found Raymond sitting with Quentin in the saloon that served warm beer. They were working on a bottle of whiskey.

"Want some breakfast?" Quentin asked.

"I ate," Dillon said. "Come on, it's time to get goin'."

"We know where Adams went?" Raymond asked.

"No, but we'll track him," Dillon said.

"You found out somethin' that makes you happy. Didn't you?" Quentin asked.

Dillon grinned and said, "Come on. I'll tell you on the way."

TWENTY-SIX

In the morning, Clint watched as the ladies broke camp. They moved well, each knowing what her job was. Even Abigail performed her assigned tasks, even if it was grudgingly.

He did what he could to help, like kicking the fire to death. He tried to help hitch the team up, but Rosemary and Jenny wouldn't hear of it and shooed him away.

When he tried to help replenish one of the water barrels from a nearby stream, Delilah and Morgan stopped him.

Finally, in the end, they all piled into the wagon, with Rosemary once again holding the reins, and Abigail next to her. It was clear Abigail did not want to be in the confines of the rear of the wagon with him, and that suited him as well.

Morgan handed him the pillow once again before they started, and he accepted it with a smile and a muttered "Thank you."

TWENTY-SEVEN

Clint was about ready to ask if he could move outside to sit beside Rosemary when the wagon stopped.

"Why are we stopping," Jenny said, and then raised her voice to ask again, "Why are we stopping?"

"Shh," Clint said.

He moved to the front of the wagon to peer out. He was able to see from between Rosemary and Abigail.

There were three riders, all men, blocking their way.

"*Hola*, señora," one of the riders said.

He seemed to be the only one who was Mexican. The other two looked like gringos.

"What's going on?" Jenny asked in a low voice.

"Looks like three men stopped us," Clint said.

"What do they want?" Morgan asked.

"I don't know," Clint said. "Just keep quiet and hand me that rifle."

Clint accepted the rifle, then went back to peering out the front.

* * *

Rosemary reined in the horses even while Abigail was saying into her ear, "Don't stop! Don't stop!"

"I don't have a choice," Rosemary hissed back. "I can't go around them."

The three riders were spread out across the road. The man in the center wore a wide sombrero and a bandolier across his chest. The other two men were Americans.

"*Hola,* señora," the man in the center said again.

"Hello," Rosemary called back. "You—uh, you're blocking the road."

"Sí, señora," the man said, "unfortunately, I am."

"Can you let us by, please?"

"Of course, of course," the man said. "But first . . . what are you carrying in the wagon?"

"Just . . . personal things," she said.

"Ah, but personal things . . . of value?" the man asked.

"Nothing of value to you, certainly," she said.

"Ah, señora," he said, "I am afraid we will have to look for ourselves, eh?"

"Tell him no," Clint said to Rosemary from right behind her. "Tell him there's a man with a rifle back here, pointing it at him."

"I—I think you should know there's a man in the back of the wagon with a rifle pointed at you."

She noticed the two men flanking the Mexican stiffen. The Mexican, however, remained relaxed.

"That is very interesting, señora," he said. "Why is the man in the wagon hiding behind your skirts?"

"He's not hiding," she said. "He was resting back there."

"Well, tell him to come out," the Mexican said, waving his arm. "We would like to meet him."

"Just tell him to move on, Rosemary," Clint said. "Tell him we don't have time for him."

Rosemary relayed the message, which the Mexican didn't like.

"I do not believe you, señora," he said. "There is no man in the wagon. I think you should—"

All three men flinched when the shot came. So did Rosemary and Abigail. The sombrero flew off the Mexican's head, eluding his hand as he grabbed for it.

"Hijo de un cabron," he swore.

"Is that proof enough for you?" she asked.

"Sí señora," he said, "it is."

"Then move aside and let us go."

The Mexican waved to the other two men, and they all moved aside. He and one man moved to their left, while the other man moved to his right.

"Tell him no matter what happens, no matter who gets shot, he'll be the first to die."

Rosemary repeated the word to the Mexican, who nodded.

Rosemary started the wagon forward and was aware of the stares of the three men as they rode by them.

Clint took the rifle and moved to the back of the wagon. This time, he allowed the barrel of the rifle to show out the back of the wagon.

They went about a mile before Rosemary reined the team in again.

"Now why are we stopping?" Jenny called out.

Rosemary stuck her head in the wagon and said, "My hands are shaking, that's why. I need a few minutes."

The women piled out of the wagon, followed by Clint, who remained ready to pull his gun from his holster in case the three men followed them.

Abigail came rushing around the wagon, shouting at Clint.

"Are you crazy? You could have got us killed."

"Those three men were going to kill you, Abigail," Clint said.

"How do you know that?" she asked. "They could have wanted anything. Directions."

"Don't be stupid, Abigail," Jenny said. "Clint saved our lives."

"At the very least," Morgan said, "he saved us from being raped."

"And how could you fire that shot between us?" Abigail went on. "You could have hurt one of us."

"Abigail," Rosemary said, "just shut up."

"No!" she shouted. "You're always telling me to shut up. Well, I won't."

Now Rosemary got in Abigail's face and shouted back, something she had never done before. "If you won't shut up," she said, "then get your stuff out of the wagon and we'll leave you here!"

"You wouldn't dare!"

"Try me, Abigail."

Abigail stared at Rosemary, who refused to avert her eyes, then turned and walked away.

Rosemary turned to Clint.

"Are we safe?" she asked.

"No," he said. "I think they'll follow us and wait for their chance."

"Like when?" she asked.

"When we amp," Clint said.

"So what do we do?" Jenny asked.

"One of two things," he said. "We can keep going, make camp when it gets dark, and wait for them to come in."

"Or?" Morgan asked.

"I can try to double-back behind them and take them."

"You mean kill them?" Rosemary asked.

"If I have to."

"Why would you have to kill them?" Delilah asked. "I mean, I just want to know why you can't just scare them away."

"I would only kill them if they wouldn't scare off," Clint said.

"Why would they come after us?" Morgan asked.

"They might think you're hiding something of value in the wagon," Clint said. "Plus, we embarrassed them. They'll want revenge for that."

"Well," Rosemary said, "you can't go after them alone. Not with one arm. So we'll have to keep going and then camp and wait for them."

"Everyone will have to do their part," Clint said.

"That's what we always do," Rosemary said.

"Okay, then," Clint said, "let's go."

TWENTY-EIGHT

The three men sat their horses and watched the wagon roll away. The Mexican, Jose Mendez—"Joe" to the other two— saw the rifle barrel sticking out the back.

"We gonna let them get away with that?" Dee Cain asked.

"No, we are not," Mendez said. "Get my sombrero, Stretch."

Stretch Conroy knew Mendez asked him to get the hat because with his long reach, he'd be able to pick it up off the ground without dismounting. He rode over and plucked the hat from the ground and brought it back to Mendez.

"Gracias," the Mexican said.

"Should we get ahead and take 'em?" Dee asked.

"No," Mendez said. "We will allow them to camp and settle in. Then we will go in and take them."

"I hope there's more women in the back of that wagon," Stretch said.

"Me, too," Dee said, "but that one handlin' the team would do for me. The other one was too old."

"Do not worry, amigos," Mendez said. "We will find out what is in the back of that wagon. I guarantee it."

Clint rode the rest of the day looking out the back of the wagon. Jenny rode up front with Rosemary, and they were keeping a watch on either side. Jenny had the rifle across her lap, although if there was any shooting to be done, Rosemary would be the one to do it.

They managed to get through the day without the Mexican and his men coming back. When they stopped to make camp, the girls went through their paces while Clint and Rosemary stood guard.

"You don't think we're safe now?" she asked him.

"No, Rosemary," he said, "men like that don't give up."

"So what are they? Highwaymen?"

"That's much too fancy a word for what they are," he replied. "They're just thieves."

"And killers?"

"When they have to be."

"They'd kill for money?"

"And for a lot less."

She looked down at the rifle in her hands.

"I don't know if I could kill anyone, Clint."

"You could," he said, "if someone was trying to kill you, or one of your friends, or family."

"Or you?"

"Well," he said, "maybe not me."

"Yes, Clint," she said, "you."

"Well," he said, "hopefully it won't come to that. Um, who's making the coffee?"

"Jenny."

"Can she make coffee?"

"Well . . ."

"I better go and help her," he said. "Keep an eye out. Also an ear."

"But what if I don't see or hear anything?"

"Don't worry," he said, "They'll wait until we're encamped before they try anything. But pay attention to Eclipse. He'll tell you if anyone's approaching."

He went to the fire to help Jenny make the coffee.

"They're bein' followed by somebody else," Quentin said. He was kneeling on the ground, eyeing some tracks.

"Who?" Raymond asked.

"I'm a good tracker, but I ain't that good," Quentin said.

"Never mind," Dillon said. "How many of them are there?"

"Three," Quentin said. "That explains what we saw farther back. The wagon tracks coming up on the three riders. They must have tried to rob the wagon." He stood up.

"And they were stopped by the Gunsmith?" Dillon asked.

"Without anybody gettin' killed?" Raymond asked.

"Who knows?" Quentin asked. "Maybe the women fought them off."

"Again . . . without anybody gettin' killed?" Raymond asked.

"Whatever happened," Quentin said, "they must be followin' them to make another try."

"When they camp," Dillon said. "That's what I'd do."

Quentin mounted up. "So what do we do?"

"Let's keep ridin'," Dillon said, "and see what happens."

"What if somebody else kills the Gunsmith before you do?" Raymond asked.

"Then I kill them," Dillon said. "It'll all come out the same."

TWENTY-NINE

Clint dropped a couple of handfuls more coffee into the pot.

"Oh my god," Jenny said. "I guess we should be glad you only have one hand to do that with."

Morgan looked up from the pot she was stirring. She was making a stew, which smelled delicious. Clint also knew that the smell would travel very far. That and the coffee. The Mexican and his partners would be able to find them easily.

"Ladies, please gather around," he said.

They all came to the fire.

"I'm sure these men will try to hit us tonight," he said.

"What if they're watching us right now?" Abigail asked. "What if they have us in their sights—"

"If they did, they probably would have fired by now. And my horse would be acting up."

"Abigail . . ." Rosemary said.

"I know," the older woman said, "shut up."

"Just listen," Rosemary said.

"The three men who stopped us today know about Rosemary and Abigail, and they know there was at least one person in the back of the wagon with a gun. We're going to use that to our advantage."

"How?" Delilah asked.

"Only three of us are going to sit around the fire," he said. "The other three will be in the bushes. With guns."

"We only have one gun," Rosemary said.

"I have more," he said. "A rifle and a handgun. Which of you can shoot, besides Rosemary?"

"I can," Jenny said.

"Can you shoot well?"

"No," she said honestly.

"That's okay. You'll probably only have to make noise. Anyone else?"

"I-I think I can," Morgan said.

"Okay, then Rosemary, Morgan, and Abigail will sit at the fire."

"Shouldn't I be in the bushes with a gun?" Rosemary asked.

"No," Clint said, "they saw you this afternoon. You and Abigail have to be at the fire."

"But . . . I can shoot," Rosemary said.

"You'll have a gun," he said. He took his Colt New Line from his belt. "This one."

"It's very small," she said.

"It'll do the trick," he said. "Besides, I expect to do most of the shooting myself."

"What about us?" Jenny asked.

"You and Morgan will have rifles," he said. "You won't fire unless I say so, and you'll fire into the air."

"But why?" Jenny asked. "How can we hit anything firing into the air?"

"You won't," Clint told her. "I don't want you to hit anything."

"But—"

"If there's any killing to be done," he said, "I'll do it."

"Then why are we going to be firing?" Jenny asked.

"To convince them that they're surrounded."

"In order to surround them, won't we have to let them into camp?" Rosemary asked.

"Yes."

"If they don't see a man at the fire," Abigail asked, "won't they be suspicious? After all, we told them there was a man in the wagon with a gun on them."

"When they see three women at the fire, they'll just think you lied to them."

"This is dangerous," Abigail said.

For once, nobody told her to shut up.

Mendez, Dee Cain, and Stretch Conroy started to move in closer to the camp, which they could smell.

"We gonna ambush 'em?" Dee asked.

"We are," Mendez said.

"Kill 'em all?" Stretch said.

"Sí," Mendez said, "but not from ambush. I want them to see us."

"So how do we do this?" Dee asked.

"I take them while they are eatin'," Mendez said. "Let them know it is us . . ."

"And then take them?" Dee asked.

"Sí."

"I want the younger one," Dee said.

"Do not worry," Mendez said. "You will have your pick."

"He has to share," Stretch said.

"I'll share," Dee said, with a grin, "but I go first."

"Quiet," Mendez said. "we are getting close."

"That smells good," Stretch said. "We get their food, too?"

"We take it all," Mendez said.

Rosemary sat with her bowl in her lap, but found she was unable to eat. However, she forced herself to, so they'd look natural.

"Eat, girls," Rosemary said. "It has to look right."

"I can't swallow," Abigail said.

"Try."

Delilah spooned some stew into her mouth.

"This is really good," she said. "When do the rest of them get to eat?"

"We'll switch off if nothing happens in a while," Rosemary said.

She put some stew in her mouth. It really was good. She put the Colt New Line down on the ground between her feet.

Clint watched the three women eat and realized how hungry he was. He was sure Jenny and Morgan were feeling the same. If something didn't happen soon, he'd let them change places with Rosemary and Delilah. As far as Abigail was concerned, he was going to keep guns out of her hands as long as he could.

Clint heard Eclipse pawing the ground at that point, and knew that somebody was approaching the camp. The question was, were they coming in from different directions, or were they together?

THIRTY

Mendez looked at the three women eating at the campfire.

"That's them," Dee said.

"And a third woman," Stretch said. "She musta been the one who shot your hat off, Joe."

"Sombrero," Mendez said. "She shot my sombrero off." At the moment, the sombrero, which now had a hole in it, was hanging on his back.

"Looks like they're eatin' stew," Stretch said. "I could use some of that."

"Do not worry," Mendez said. "Everything they have will be ours."

"How do we do this?" Dee asked.

Mendez drew his gun. "We walk in and let them know we are here," he said.

"Just like that?" Dee asked.

"Just like that," Mendez said. "Draw your guns, amigos."

* * * *

When the three men walked into camp Rosemary kept herself from grabbing the Colt New Line.

"Oh!" Abigail said.

"Easy, girls," Rosemary said.

"Ladies," Mendez said, "we meet again!"

All three men had guns in their hands.

"What do we do?" Abigail hissed.

"Just wait . . ." Rosemary said.

"And we meet the third lady," Mendez said. "The one who likes to shoot at sombreros."

"I was aiming at your head," Delilah said.

Mendez laughed, followed by the other two men.

"Is that stew?" Stretch asked.

"It is," Rosemary said. "Unfortunately, there's just enough for us."

"Oh, that won't be a problem," Mendez said. "Ladies, please put your bowls down and stand up."

Rosemary put her bowl down between her feet and grabbed the Colt New Line.

As the three men moved on the three women around the fire, Clint stepped out of the bushes. He hoped Rosemary wouldn't use that gun until he said so.

"Hold it there," he said.

Mendez and the other two men turned their heads to look at him.

Rosemary picked up the gun and held it in her lap.

"Shoot them!" Abigail hissed.

"Not 'til Clint says so."

"And who is this?" Mendez asked. "So, there really was a man in the back of the wagon?"

"That's right," Clint said. "I shot off your sombrero. And I meant to. I wasn't aiming at your head."

"It was a nice shot," Mendez said.

"Thanks."

"So, you are charged with protecting these women?" the Mexican asked.

"That's right. So you and your boys just put your guns down. You're covered."

"By you?"

"No," Clint said. "Fire one shot!" he called.

Both Jenny and Morgan fired a shot into the air. The three men flinched.

"You're surrounded," Clint said. "And covered."

Mendez looked at Rosemary. She was holding the New Line in both hands, pointing it at him.

"Your move, señor," Clint said.

•

Mendez considered the situation. There were four people in camp, two with guns. The man's gun was still in his holster. He didn't know how many more there were in the bushes, but they all had to be able to fit into one wagon. That meant there couldn't be that many more.

"Amigo," Mendez said, "your gun is still holstered, and I do not believe we are surrounded. Oh, there may be two or three people in the bushes, but I believe you are bluffing."

Great, Clint thought. He's going to make me prove it.

"What's your name, amigo?" Clint asked.

"Jose Mendez," the Mexican said, "but you can call me Joe."

"Well, Joe, this is not a good situation. That lady there has a gun pointed at you."

"She will not pull the trigger," Mendez said, "but we will."

"And so will I," Clint said.

"Three against one, amigo," Mendez said. "Your move."

THIRTY-ONE

Clint knew the odds were against him, and normally that wouldn't have bothered him. But he didn't know if he could take them—not left-handed. And he didn't think the women in the bushes would be any help.

"All right," he said. "All right."

"Hold it!" Rosemary said, standing up. "Girls, come on out!"

Jenny and Morgan came out, pointing their rifles at the three men.

"It's four against three, Mr. Mendez," Rosemary said. "We're not very good with these guns, but we're bound to hit something, I think."

Mendez, Dee, and Stretch looked around them.

"Joe?" Dee said.

Abigail had brought her knees up to her chest, was trying to make herself as small a target as possible. Delilah simply sat still.

Mendez looked at Clint.

"What is your name, amigo?" he asked.

"Clint Adams."

"Adams?" Dee asked.

"The Gunsmith?" Stretch said.

"That's right."

"And these women are under your protection?" Mendez asked.

"It seems to me they can protect themselves," Clint said, "but I am at their disposal."

"We did not know," Mendez said.

"Well, now you do," Clint said. "Leave these women alone."

Mendez lowered his gun. So did the other two.

"Leave the guns," Clint said, deciding to push it.

"What?" Mendez said.

"Leave the guns, amigo," Clint said, "or use them."

Mendez froze. For a moment, Clint thought he'd gone too far.

"Joe?" Stretch said. "He wasn't asking, he was telling." He and Dee Cain clearly wanted to lay their weapons down.

"Very well," Mendez said.

The three men put their guns on the ground.

"Now walk away, amigos, and don't come back."

Mendez turned and walked away, followed by Cain and Stretch.

Rosemary lowered her arm as if the gun weighed a hundred pounds.

"Can we eat now?" Jenny asked.

THIRTY-TWO

They all sat around the fire, eating stew.

"What if they go to their horses for their rifles and come back?" Abigail asked.

"They know who Clint is now," Rosemary said. "They won't be back."

"But . . . he couldn't have beaten them. Not with his left hand."

"They don't know that," Jenny said.

"They might come back to find out," Abigail said.

"They won't," Clint said. "They're done. They'll move on to find easier prey."

"So we're safe?" Abigail asked.

"From them," Clint pointed out. "But there are other men out there like those."

"How does anyone live out here?" Abigail asked. "We should have stayed in St. Louis, where we were safe."

"There are bad men in St. Louis, Abigail," Clint said.

"Not like this," she said. "Not animals who would rape or kill us."

"I'm afraid there are animals like that all over."

Jenny tried to put her arm around Abigail, but the older woman shrunk away. She remained silent for the rest of the meal.

Clint decided to set watches for the night.

"I'll go first," he told Rosemary, "then you, then Jenny, then either Morgan or Delilah."

"I'll tell them to take a watch together," she said.

"What about Abigail?" Clint asked.

"I don't think she'd be very good as a lookout," she said.

"You're probably right," he said.

"Are you having second thoughts about them coming back?" she asked.

"No," he said. "I just think we should be careful, that's all. You go ahead and get some sleep."

"Can I tell you something?"

"Sure."

"I was really scared."

"That's okay," he said. "Most people would have been."

"But I would have shot him."

"I know you would've," he said. "Sleep well."

Morgan and Delilah took the last watch together, then woke Clint at first light.

"Coffee," he said, grabbing the pot. It was almost empty so he made a new one. It was ready by the time Rosemary had breakfast going in a pan.

"Everybody sleep okay?" Clint asked.

"How could we?" Abigail asked. "We were waiting to be murdered in our sleep."

"I slept fine," Jenny said.

"So did I," Rosemary said. "I felt . . . safer."

They sat around the fire and had breakfast. Clint then poured the remnants of the coffeepot over the fire. It was Morgan's turn to clean up. She stowed the pots and pans and utensils in the wagon.

Clint kept a sharp eye out. He didn't expect Mendez and his two partners to return, but if they did he wanted to be ready.

The coast was clear by the time they were ready to move on. Clint could move his arm, but there was still no movement on his hand. If he'd had to draw left-handed the night before, he wasn't sure what would have happened. Rosemary had pretty much saved him from finding out by calling the women out of the bushes. And it was the second time his name and reputation had kept the situation from turning deadly.

But he couldn't count on it to work a third time.

THIRTY-THREE

Dillon, Raymond and Quentin came upon the camp. Quentin put his hand over the fire ashes.

"Still warm," he said. "And a lot of tracks here. Too many to just be them."

"Whoever was tailing them caught up," Dillon said. "No gunplay?"

"Can't tell for sure, but it doesn't look like there are any bodies around," Raymond said.

"And no sign that any were dragged away," Quentin said. "And no shallow graves around."

"A standoff?" Dillon said.

"Maybe," Quentin said.

"Did they follow them after this?" Dillon asked.

"Doesn't look like it, but I'll know better when we move on. I'll be able to see if they're still being tailed."

"If Adams stood off three guns," Raymond said, "maybe he ain't so hurt anymore?"

"We'll find out when we catch up to them," Dillon said.

"We shoulda caught them by now," Raymond said.

"We were being careful about their tail," Quentin said.

"If they're not following them anymore, we'll be able to move in," Dillon said.

"What if we found them?" Quentin asked, mounting up again. Dillon and Raymond had been looking down at him from their horses. "We could join forces. Six against the Gunsmith."

"We don't need six," Dillon said. "In fact, I might not even need you fellas. Unless the women have guns. Then you can take care of them."

"I ain't gonna shoot no women," Raymond said.

"You will," Quentin said, "if they're shootin' at you."

"I don't know . . ." Raymond said, riding off.

Quentin looked at Dillon. "Where'd you find this one?"

"He'll learn," Dillon said.

"I just hope he don't learn the hard way," Quentin said. "By one of them women putting a bullet into him."

THIRTY-FOUR

The wagon rode into the town of Clear Creek late in the day; they decided they'd stay there for the night and re-stock in the morning with whatever they needed. They hadn't been traveling that long, so they didn't need that much more in the way of supplies.

Rosemary actually wanted to see if the town had a doctor who could look at Clint's arm, maybe get a new opinion.

They stopped the wagon in front of a small hotel. Once again, Rosemary decided the five women would share two rooms. Clint would be able to afford his own very easily.

Clint, Rosemary, Delilah, and Abigail went into the hotel. Jenny and Morgan took the wagon and Eclipse to the livery stable. They agreed to meet in the lobby and get something to eat together.

They checked in and carried whatever gear they had to their rooms. Rosemary decided to again room with Abigail, if only to keep the woman's mouth under control.

Clint carried his saddlebags and rifle in his one good hand and set them down outside the door to fit the key in the lock. Once he had it open, he picked up his gear again and went inside.

He dropped the saddlebags and rifle into a corner and sat on the bed. He was able to lift his arm to shoulder length and extend it out in front of him, but the hand just hung loosely at the end. He thought he felt some tingling in the hand when he woke up, but it did not reoccur during the day, so he started to think he'd imagined it. Tingling, the doctor had said, would be good. At least it would be some kind of feeling.

He stared down at his hand, keeping it in his lap, willing it to move, or even to tingle. But there was nothing.

He left the room and went down to the lobby to meet the others.

His hand may have not been moving, but he sure was hungry.

He found Rosemary, Delilah, and Abigail waiting in the lobby.

"I checked with the desk clerk for a good place to eat," Rosemary said. "He recommended a café down the street."

"I'm not going to be particular today," Clint said. "As long as they can burn a steak."

They stepped outside to wait for Jenny and Morgan.

"How's your hand?" Rosemary asked.

"The same."

"No movement or feeling at all?" she asked.

"No."

"I also asked the desk clerk if the town had a doctor," she said. "He said yes."

"This is a little bit of a town, Rosemary," he said. "I doubt the doctor here would know more than Doc Jacobs did."

"There's no harm in checking with him, is there?" she asked.

"Probably not," he agreed.

Jenny and Morgan appeared at that point and they all walked to the café down the street.

They did indeed know how to fire a steak. In fact, they burned them good. Clint, Rosemary, and Jenny ordered steaks and got them well done. Abigail and Morgan ordered chicken, while Delilah had the beef stew.

After they finished eating Rosemary—who had once again cut Clint's meat for him—said, "I'm going to go to the doctor with Clint. Jenny, you and Delilah go over to the general store and replenish our supplies. It shouldn't take much."

"What should we do?" Abigail asked.

"You and Morgan go to the livery, ask the man to check that wheel and make sure it's still secure."

"But, why do we—"

"We'll take care of it, Rosemary," Morgan said. "Don't worry."

"When we're all done, we can go to our rooms and get some rest," Rosemary said. "We'll be leaving again at first light."

They all nodded, except for Abigail. Out in front of the café, they split up.

"How much longer can you put up with it?" Clint asked as they went in search of the doctor.

"Put up with what?"

"Abigail, and her attitude."

"We left St. Louis together, Clint," she said. "We have to stay together. That's just the way it is."

"And what if she decided to leave, on her own?" he asked.

"Then that would be her decision," Rosemary said. "I wouldn't stand in her way. Here it is."

They stopped in front of a shingle that read: DOCTOR E. SHALE

"Rosemary—"

"Would you just do this for me?" she asked.

He sighed. "All right, yes. Let's go in."

"Thank you."

They opened the door and stepped inside. Immediately, Clint smelled the whiskey, and the odor of stale sweat.

"Oh, what is that?" she asked.

"Hopefully," he said, "it's not our doctor."

They were in an office, a small, roll-top desk up against one wall. There was another door, which they imagined led to a surgery.

"Shall we?" he asked.

She looked as if she had changed her mind, but she nodded and they went in.

THIRTY-FIVE

The man was lying facedown in a pool of whiskey. On the floor. An empty bottle was lying next to him.

"I wonder if this is Doctor Shale?" Clint asked.

"Oh, it can't be," she said.

"Why not?"

"Because he's a doctor."

"Doc Holliday was a dentist, and he was a drunk," Clint said.

"You knew Doc Holliday?" she asked.

"I did."

"Well . . . well . . . this must be different," she said. "I mean . . . a doctor?"

"Then where is he?" Clint asked. "Where is the doctor?"

"I don't know," she said, "but what do we do about . . . him?" She pointed at the man on the floor.

"Well," he said, "first let's keep him from drowning in whiskey."

Clint reached down and turned the man over onto his back. They were surprised to see that he was young, maybe in his thirties.

"Now what?" she asked.

"Well, we could just leave."

"But he needs help."

"He needs more help than we can give him," Clint commented.

"I mean, right now."

"Okay," Clint said. "We can clean him up, wake him up, and find out who he is. Maybe he knows where the doctor went."

"Okay," she said. "Let's do that."

"First, we need some water . . ."

When the man opened his eyes, he stared up at them, frowning.

"What happened?" he asked. "Who are you?"

"I'm Clint, and this is Rosemary," he said. "We came in looking for the doctor and found you facedown in a pool of whiskey."

"We saved you from drowning," she said, "and cleaned you up. How do you feel?"

"Awful," he said. "So you have a drink?"

"No," she said. "My God, that's how you got in this condition."

"Believe me, I know how I got this way," he said. "I'm a doctor."

That stunned Rosemary. Clint could see that.

"You're . . . a doctor? Are you . . . the doctor? I mean, Doctor Shale?"

"That's me," he said, rubbing his face and sitting up. "But I'm closed today."

"Just today?" Clint asked.

"Yes, look," Shale said, hanging his head, "I'm just not . . . in any condition . . ."

"Coffee," Clint said.

"What?"

"You need coffee," Clint said. "Is there a kitchen here?"

"Yeah, in the back, but—"

"Make some coffee, Rosemary," Clint said. "For all of us."

"A-all right."

As she left the room, Shale asked, "Is she your wife?"

"No, we're just friends," Clint said.

"Lovely woman."

"Yes, she is."

Shale looked down at himself and said, "Oh God. I should wash up." He stood up. "You did come here looking for treatment, right?"

"Yes."

"Well . . . let me wash up, and then have some of that coffee," Shale said, "and we'll see."

THIRTY-SIX

They got Shale cleaned up and put a couple of cups of coffee into him. He stared at them with bloodshot eyes, as if seeing them for the first time.

"Say, you're very pretty," he said to Rosemary.

"Thank you."

"I didn't get your names, though."

"Clint and Rosemary," she said.

"I'm Ethan Shale."

"*Doctor* Ethan Shale, right?" Rosemary asked, still dubious.

"Yes," he said, "I know it's hard to believe considering the condition you found me in, but I am the town doctor."

"What happened to you?" Rosemary asked.

"That's a fair question," the doctor said. "It was a woman. Need I say more?"

"Yes," Rosemary said.

"No," Clint said. "That's enough."

Rosemary looked at Clint, but did not press the issue.

"Well," the doctor said, "maybe you folks should tell me why you're here?"

Clint rolled up his sleeve and explained his injury to Doctor Shale.

"Can I have your hand, please?" Shale asked.

Clint extended it. The doctor felt the hand, moved the fingers, asked about pain.

"You mind if I see the wound itself?" he asked then.

"No, go ahead."

Shale unwrapped the wound with remarkable steady hands, considering how they'd found him.

He leaned in to look at the wound, the stitching, to poke a bit at the edges, causing Clint some pain.

"Sorry," he said.

"That's fine," Clint said.

"Let me see you move the arm?"

Clint moved his arm up and down, in a circular fashion, while the doctor asked for reports of pain.

"Now hold your arm out and try to move your fingers, please."

Clint did so. His fingers did not move at all, but the doctor seemed to be more concerned with his wrist and his forearm.

Shale newly wrapped the arm with care and then sat back.

"What's the verdict, Doctor?" Rosemary asked.

"Well, the hand and fingers seem to be fine," Shale said.

"Fine?" she asked.

"I'm finding dexterity in the hand."

"Which means what?" Clint asked.

"Well, that mechanically, the hand is fine."

"Then why can't I move it?"

"I don't think your hand is getting the message."

"What?"

"From your forearm," he said, "or your brain. See, your brain sends a message to your hand to move." The doctor leaned forward and waved his hand over Clint's forearm. "I don't think the message is getting past here."

"What does that mean?" Rosemary asked.

"Let's say the tendons in your arm are like telegraph wires," Shale said. "I'm sayin' that one of the wires has been cut."

"But . . . with a telegraph wire you can fix it," Rosemary said.

"Exactly."

"Are you saying you can fix it?" Clint asked.

"Well, theoretically, with surgery, I should be able to reattach the tendon."

"Well, that's great," Clint said. "When can you do it?"

"Who, whoa," Shale said, sitting back, "I should have said that theoretically, *someone* should be able to reattach the tendons."

"Someone?" Clint asked.

"Someone better than me."

"The doctor in Big Rock didn't mention any of this," Rosemary said.

"Doctor Jacobs?"

She nodded.

"He's a good man, but this would be beyond him," Shale said.

"And beyond you?" Clint asked.

"Well . . . I have the knowledge. I mean, I went to medical school in the East, learned a lot of new procedures that somebody like Doc Jacobs wouldn't know, but . . ."

"But what?" Clint asked.

"Would you want to put your arm in the hands of the man you found facedown on the floor an hour ago?" Shale asked.

"I'd want to put myself in the hands of a good doctor who knows what he's doing," Clint said.

"You could probably find a doctor in another town . . . or back East . . ."

"I don't have the time," Clint said.

"Why not?"

"I may not live that long, Doctor."

Shale scoffed.

"This wound is not fatal—"

"It is to me," Clint said.

"I don't understand."

"I told you my name is Clint," Clint said. "My full name is Clint Adams."

"Clint . . . Adams?" The doctor sat back, stared at Clint. "I see," he said finally, "I see now what you mean."

"Can you do it, Doctor?" Rosemary asked.

The doctor ran his hands over his face, frowned when he felt the stubble there.

"It could make you famous—" Rosemary started.

"No, no," Shale said, waving her off, "that doesn't come into play in my decision. In fact, I'm sure Mr. Adams would not want the word to get out."

"No, I wouldn't."

"No," Shale said, "but there would be a certain amount of personal satisfaction for me . . ."

"And I'd pay you, of course," Clint said. "Anything."

"Anything within reason," Rosemary said.

"No," Clint said, looking the doctor in the eye, "anything!"

THIRTY-SEVEN

"We're what?" Abigail asked.

"Not we," Rosemary said, "me."

They were all gathered in one of the hotel rooms—the one Rosemary was sharing with Abigail.

"But you can't abandon us," Abigail said.

"I'm not abandoning anyone," Rosemary said. "Clint is going to have a surgery on his arm. I want to be here to see if it works. And to support him. I'll join you all in California."

"No," Jenny said.

"What?" Rosemary asked.

They all turned and looked at the youngest of the group.

"If you're staying," Jenny said, "I'm staying, too. I want to support him, also."

"Well," Morgan said, "I might as well stay, too."

"If you're all staying," Delilah said, "I am, too. I say we all stick together."

"You're all crazy," Abigail said. "We don't owe this man anything just because he fixed a wheel."

"He did more than that," Rosemary said.

"He saved us from those men," Jenny said. "Risked his life."

"We'll still go to California," Morgan said. "Just later."

"Where is he?" Jenny asked Rosemary.

"In his room."

"You better go and tell him that we'll support him," Jenny said. "All of us."

"Unless Abigail wants to take the wagon and go ahead alone," Morgan said.

"Don't be ridiculous!" Abigail said. "You all know I can't and won't do that."

"Then it's settled," Jenny said with a big smile. "We're all staying."

"When will the surgery be done?" Morgan asked.

"We don't know that yet," Rosemary said. "It's up to the doctor."

"Is there a problem?" Delilah asked.

"There might be one."

"What is it?" Jenny asked.

"Well," Rosemary said, "the doctor is, uh kind of a drunk."

Clint was in his room, lying on the bed with his boots off, his gun hanging on the bedpost as usual, but on the left side.

He was staring at the cracks in the ceiling, thinking of each as tendons in his arm. Doctor Shale said he could open Clint's arm and reattach the tendon that was damaged. Then they'd just have to wait and see if movement returned to his hand.

There was no guarantee.

Doctor Shale sat in his office, thinking about what the day had brought. His drunken stupor had begun the night before, and apparently lasted until morning. Or until Clint Adams and the woman, Rosemary, found him and revived him.

Revived.

Could fixing the Gunsmith's arm revive him, as well? Perhaps revive his whole life?

It wouldn't bring back the woman he loved, who had left him, but it might just bring him back to life.

Rosemary knocked on Clint's door. When he opened the door, he looked tired.

"I'm sorry, were you asleep?"

"No," he said, "counting cracks in the ceiling. Come on in."

He let her enter and closed the door. She turned to face him.

"I wanted to tell you that we all decided to stay and see you through this."

He smiled. "That's really nice, but there's no need for that," he said. "You ladies have a trip to finish—"

"We can put it off for a few days," she said, "or a while. However long it takes you to heal."

"Rosemary—"

"Please," she said, "this is something we'd like to do. We still feel responsible for the way you got hurt. We'd like to know that you're going to be all right."

"Well . . . okay," he said. "Thanks. It would be nice to have some support."

He felt sure he would have been fine without them, but for some reason this seemed to be something that they needed. All but Abigail.

THIRTY-EIGHT

Dillon stared at the town ahead.

"Small town," he said.

"We shoulda took them on the trail," Raymond said.

"Town's better," Dillon said.

"Why?" Raymond asked.

"More witnesses," Quentin said.

"You want witnesses when you kill a man?" Raymond asked.

"When it's a fair fight, you do," Quentin said.

"And this is gonna be a fair fight," Dillon said.

"What if his right hand ain't hurt. Like they said?" Raymond asked. "What then? You still gonna try him?"

"We'll have to see," Dillon said.

"We goin' in?" Raymond asked.

"We're goin' in," Dillon said. "We're only about half a day behind them. They can't be too settled."

"Shouldn't we go in one at a time?" Raymond asked.

"No," Dillon said. "Three strangers riding in one at a

time might even attract more attention than three men riding in separately. Let's go."

The three men started their horses forward.

Clint entered the sheriff's office and found it empty. He
took a look into the cellblock, found two cells, doors wide
open. When he stepped back into the office, a man was
coming in. He wore a badge and looked like he was in his
late twenties.

"Sheriff?" he asked.

"Deputy," the man said, "but I guess I'm the temporary
sheriff."

"Where's the regular one?"

"He had to leave town, go to the county seat," the deputy said. He walked around behind the desk, but didn't sit.
"My name's Web Kane."

"Clint Adams."

The deputy rocked back on his heels. "The Gunsmith?"

"That's right."

"In this town? Why?"

"Just passing through," Clint said. "I'm escorting five
women traveling in a wagon."

"Five women?"

"They were traveling alone for a while, and then we
met up," Clint said. "I thought they needed some protection."

"Well, lucky for them," Kane said. "How long will you
be stayin' in town?"

"The women need some rest," Clint said. "Two or
three days, I guess."

"You ain't here lookin' for anybody, are you, Mr.

Adams?" Kane asked. "I mean, you ain't lookin' for trouble?"

"Deputy," Clint said, "I'm never looking for trouble."

Clint went back to the hotel and found Jenny in the lobby.

"You told us to keep watching the street," she said.

"That's right," he said. "I told you to take turns."

"Well, it's my turn and I saw three men ride into town."

"When?"

"A few minutes ago."

"Half a day behind us," he said. "They could have been following our trail."

"But it wasn't the same three men," she said. "The Mexican and the other two. Maybe they're just passing through?"

"We came to town today, and then they come in? Too much of a coincidence for a small town like this."

"So what do we do?"

"We'll just have to keep an eye out for them," Clint said.

"What about the sheriff?"

"He's out of town," Clint said. "There's only a young deputy."

"Can he help?"

"If he's any good at his job," Clint said, "which I doubt."

"We need guns," she said.

"No," Clint said. "No guns. In fact, none of you should even be seen with me outside the hotel."

"Why not?"

"If there's shooting on the street, you might get hurt."

"But we have to back you up."

"No, you don't," Clint said. "The five of you just have to stay out of the way, and safe. Leave the rest to me."

THIRTY-NINE

Clint figured if the three men were after him, they were going to take a look around town, first. Before they did anything they'd have to check out how much law was in town. So he was pretty safe for the night. Still, he took precautions. He laid the pitcher and basin on the windowsill, and was jamming the back of a chair underneath the doorknob when there was a knock.

It was difficult to open the door and hold his gun at the same time, so he stuck the gun in his belt and then opened it. It was Rosemary.

"May I come in?" she asked.

"Sure."

She stepped in and he closed the door. She looked at the chair standing next to him.

"Oh, I was just locking up for the night," he said, "being careful." He indicated the windowsill, where the pitcher and basin were. "I was putting the back of the chair beneath the doorknob."

"Well, go ahead and lock up, then," she said, sitting on the bed. "I wasn't planning on leaving."

He stared at her for a moment, then stuck the back of the chair beneath the knob.

Rosemary removed Clint's shirt, careful not to jostle his right arm.

"You carry this well when you're dressed," she said. "Nobody can tell you have an injured arm."

"If they can tell, I'd be dead," he said.

"What about you wearing the gun with the butt forward?" she asked. "Is that necessarily a giveaway?"

"No," he said. "I've known a few men who have worn it that way, even though they're right-handed. I've never understood it, though."

He was lying on his back on the bed; she was next to him, still fully dressed. She undid his belt and unbuttoned his pants. He lifted his hips so she could slip them off. He had already removed his boots—with difficulty—before she got there.

She discarded the pants and lay back down next to him. She traced a pattern over his chest with her fingers, moved them down to his belly, around his belly button. "You're a fascinating man," she said. "I thought that from the start."

"Even before the wagon fell on me?"

"Oh yes," she said, "even before then. How did you know how to fix the wagon? How did you know what a— what did you call it?"

"A carter key?"

"Yes, how did you know what a carter key was?"

"I used to ride around in my own wagon," he said. "Had to fix it plenty of times."

"What kind of wagon?"

"A gunsmithing wagon," he said.

"You mean you really are a gunsmith?"

"Oh yes," he said. "I plied my trade for a little while, but eventually I gave the wagon up. That's when I simply started riding around the country, from one end to the other sometimes."

"That must be wonderful," she said, "but lonely, sometimes?"

"Sometimes," he said. "Mostly, I like it."

She slid her hand into his underwear, found him hardening. Hooking her fingers into the cloth, she dragged it down over his legs. He was totally naked.

"You're also a beautiful man," she said, sliding her fingertips over the smooth skin of his hard shaft.

"Won't the others wonder where you are?" he asked.

"I'm sharing my room with Abigail," she said, "and she will know where I am."

He looked at her, reached for her shirt with his left hand.

"I'll do it," she said.

"Stand up and let me watch you."

She stood by the bed and undressed. She had a sleek body, small but round breasts, slender hips, long legs. She turned for him, showing her rounded, dimpled butt, the beautiful line of her back.

Her hair was up and she let it down. It shimmered. He grew harder, still.

"Come to bed," he said.

"You have to promise you'll take it easy," she said.

"I promise I won't hurt you, Rosemary."

"Silly, I'm worried about you hurting yourself," she said. "Or me hurting you." She got into bed next to him, pressing her naked hip against his. "I've been wanting this since we met, and I just might tear you to pieces."

FORTY

Dillon, Raymond, and Quentin found a saloon with cold beer and hardboiled eggs on the bar.

"How many other saloons in town?" Dillon asked the bartender.

"One," the man said, "but this is the best one."

"What's the other one got on the bar?" Quentin asked.

"Peanuts," the bartender said.

"I'll take the eggs," Raymond said.

"Penny a piece," the bartender said.

"We'll take three each, and a beer," Dillon said.

"Comin' up."

The bartender drew them three beers. They carried them to a table with the eggs. There were only three other men in the place, and they ignored the strangers. There was one bored-looking saloon girl, a brunette in her late twenties. Or maybe she was younger and only looked like she was in her late twenties.

"Come here, sweetie," Dillon said.

She rolled her eyes and walked over.

"Don't worry," Dillon said, "you're too skinny for me to want anything from you but answers."

"Whaddaya wanna know?"

"Who's the law in this town?"

"Sheriff Hughes."

"Where is he?"

"He's not in town," she said. "Had to go to the county seat."

"How far is that?"

"Forty miles."

"Who'd he leave in charge?"

"His deputy."

"Any good."

"Ain't worth a damn," she said, "but we ain't got a bank, if that's what you're thinkin'."

"A bank?" Dillon asked. "Why would we be interested in a bank?"

"You would if you were bank robbers."

"Well," Quentin said, "we ain't."

"What are ya here for, then?" she asked.

"To ask questions," Dillon said, "not to answer them, sweetie. Thanks. You can go."

She looked at all three of them.

"You ain't too skinny for me," Raymond said with a leer.

She rolled her eyes and walked away.

"We only got one deputy to deal with," Dillon said, "and even the saloon girl says he's nothin'."

"So we go now?" Raymond asked. "Take the Gunsmith in his hotel?"

"No," Dillon said, "we take him on the street tomorrow, in front of everyone."

"Everyone?" Quentin asked. "There ain't nobody in this town, Dillon."

"I only need a few witnesses," Dillon said.

"So, in the mornin'?" Raymond asked.

"No," Dillon said, "I want to check on the deputy, first."

"But the girl—" Raymond said.

"You wanna risk your life on the word of a saloon girl?"

"I don't," Quentin said.

"So we check out the deputy," Dillon said.

"When?" Raymond asked.

The batwings opened at that moment and a man wearing a badge walked in.

"How about right now?" Dillon asked.

"We take 'im?" Raymond asked.

"We check him out," Dillon said. "Just stay seated, boys."

Dillon stood up and walked to the bar, where the deputy was standing.

FORTY-ONE

Rosemary straddled Clint, leaned down to press her breasts into his face. He nibbled on her pink nipples as she sat up, and used his left hand to stroke and tug on them. He lifted his right arm at one point, but his hand was useless. He let it fall back to the bed.

"Don't worry," she said, kissing him tenderly, "it's all right."

She kissed his mouth, his face, his neck, his chest, worked her way down over his belly, and then lower still. She nuzzled his hard cock, held it in her hands, stroked it, then licked it. She worked her way up and down the shaft, wetting him, then opened her mouth and took the bulging head of his penis inside. Her mouth was hot and wet and he groaned and lifted his hips as she started to suck. With his one good hand, he reached down and cupped her head as she sucked him avidly.

* * *

Dillon stood next to the deputy and asked for a beer. The deputy already had one.

"How's it going, Web?" the bartender asked.

"Okay, I guess," Deputy Kane said.

"When's the sheriff gettin' back?"

"Few days."

"Been quiet."

"Hope it stays that way," Kane said.

"Not much excitement in this town?" Dillon asked the two men.

"No, sir," Kane said. "Stay pretty quiet around here."

"I just rode in, but I already heard somethin', was wonderin' if it was true."

"What's that?" the bartender asked.

"I heard the Gunsmith was in town."

"What?" the bartender asked. "Mister, if Clint Adams was in town, believe me, I'd know it."

Kane turned to face Dillon. "Where'd you hear that, mister?"

"Just around."

"Naw," Kane said, "that word ain't goin' around."

"It's ain't?"

"I know that for sure."

"Then maybe you know for sure that he's here, too," Dillon said.

"Kane?" the bartender asked. "Is that true?"

"Quiet, Rufus," Kane said. "Mister, we just finished tellin' you how quiet this little town is. We aim to keep it that way."

"I ain't lookin' for trouble, Deputy," Dillon said. "I was just tellin' you what I heard."

"And I'm sayin' you didn't hear that in this town."

Dillon frowned. "Are you callin' me a liar?"

"I ain't sayin' that," Kane replied. "But I am sayin' you're mistaken."

Dillon stared at the young deputy. He didn't come to town to kill a lawman, and killing this one would warn Adams.

"Okay, Deputy," he said, "have it your way. I was mistaken."

"And I'd appreciate it if you wouldn't be passin' false information like that around, anymore."

"Sure, Deputy," Dillon said, picking up his beer, "have it your way."

He walked back to his table to rejoin his friends.

"That was pretty good, Web," the bartender said. "The sheriff'd be proud of you."

"Yeah, thanks."

The man leaned in and asked, "Is it true? Is the Gunsmith in town?"

"Shut up, Rufus," Kane said, and left.

"Hot damn!" Rufus said, and began to look around for somebody to tell.

FORTY-TWO

Rosemary sucked him until he almost exploded in her mouth, then released him, kissed his belly, fondled his sack for a few moments, then mounted him and took him inside. If her mouth had been hot, her pussy was like molten lava.

"Ahhhhh," Clint went, closing his eyes.

"Oooh," she said as he filled her up.

He used his hand to roam her body, run over her smooth skin, knead it, pinch it. He felt her rounded ass, moved his hand up her back as she moved on him.

"Oh, yes," she said. "Mmmm, I'm just going to . . . do this for a while . . ."

"Take your time," he told her. "We've . . . got all night . . ."

She rode his cock for a few minutes. He found her rhythm and moved with her until it was almost like a dance. Then, at one point, she brought her hand down on the bed, and onto his right arm.

"Ow!" he cried out, and pulled his arm away.

"Omigod!" she yelled. "I'm so sorry."

His erection was gone in an instant. She rolled off him and he sat up and grabbed his arm, cradled it, staring at his hand.

"Damn, that hurt."

"I'm sorry—"

"No," he said, "you don't understand. It hurt in my hand."

"Did—did your fingers move?"

"No, but I had some feeling there!"

"Oh, Clint!" she said. "That's wonderful. You'll have to tell the doctor tomorrow."

He pulled her to him and kissed her.

"You mean—can you still?"

He looked down and she followed his eyes. His penis was getting hard again. "It'll take more than a little pain in the arm to distract me from you," he said, nuzzling her neck.

In his ear, she said, "I promise to be very, very careful with you."

"Then get back to what you were doing, girl," he told her.

"Jesus," Raymond said when he woke up the next morning, "no whorehouse. Can you believe it?"

"Shut up," Quentin said from the next bed.

They were sharing a room, while Dillon had taken his own.

"Couldn't even get that skinny saloon girl to come up last night," Raymond continued to complain.

"Guess she had better taste than that," Quentin said, from beneath the covers.

"I need some breakfast."

"Well, go get it!" Quentin said. "Leave me be."

While he dressed, Raymond asked, "When did Dillon say we wuz gonna kill the Gunsmith?"

"He didn't say!" Quentin snapped. "Why don't you go wake him up and ask him?"

Raymond finished dressing and left the room, grumbling.

Dillon woke and checked the action on his gun, found that it worked smoothly. He sat on the edge of the bed naked, cleaning his gun and thinking of the girl, Candy. When this was all over, he was going to go back to that town.

If he could only remember the name of it.

When he woke the next morning Clint's arm was sore from where she had leaned on it, but that didn't matter to him. He sat on the edge of the bed and stared down at the hand, willing it to move. It didn't, but he was still optimistic about what the doctor had said, and what he'd felt last night. Pain in his hand was a big improvement.

He turned and looked at Rosemary. She was lying with her back to him, her knees curled up, her butt nicely rounded. He got back into bed and was able to lie on his left side, letting his penis ride in the crack between her butt cheeks.

"Mmmm," she said, "that's the way to wake a girl up."

"I'm hungry," he said.

"Let me turn over."

"No," he said. "I mean for food."

She reached behind her and took him in her hand, squeezing tightly.

"This doesn't feel like hungry for food," she said.

"Well, okay, then," he said. "Turn over."

"No," she said, moving her legs, "let's do it this way . . ."

FORTY-THREE

Raymond decided not to wake Dillon. He went down to find breakfast by himself.

Quentin couldn't fall back to sleep after Raymond left, so he got dressed and left his room.

Dillon got hungry, so he dressed, strapped on his gun, and left his room. In the hall, he saw Quentin coming out of his.

"Breakfast?" Dillon asked.

"That idiot woke me up, bitchin' about no whorehouse," Quentin said. "Yeah, let's get somethin' to eat."

The three men were staying at the other hotel in town, across the street and down the block from the one Clint and the women were staying in.

When Clint and Rosemary came out of the hotel, Raymond was already in a small restaurant having breakfast.

And they didn't see Dillon and Quentin leaving their hotel.

"Should we wake the others?" he asked.

"No," she said, "let them sleep. I'd like to have breakfast just with you."

"Well, there can't be too many places in a town this size," he said.

She put her hand on his arm—his left arm—to stop him.

"What if you're right? There aren't many places to eat, and we run into . . . those men?"

"I've got to run into them sooner or later," Clint said. "If we do, you make sure you hit the floor if there's any shooting."

"If?" she asked.

"When," he said.

Deputy Web Kane came out of the sheriff's office in time to see Clint and Rosemary walking down the street. He hurried to catch them.

"Mr. Adams?"

They turned to face him.

"I'm glad I caught you," Kane said. "There's a man, a very big man, he was in the bar last night askin' about you."

"Asking what?"

"He said he heard you were in town," he said. "He couldn't have heard it from anyone. I didn't tell anyone."

"He could have got it from the desk clerk," Clint said, "but it's more likely he tracked us here."

"Tracked you?"

"Our wagon," Clint said. "Very easy to follow."

"And what's he want?"

"What do they all want, Deputy?"

"A chance at the Gunsmith?"

Clint nodded.

"But . . . your arm."

"How did you—" Rosemary said, then stopped.

"The way you hold it," Kane said. "It's not obvious, but you have your gun in your holster butt forward. And I saw you go to the doctor's office."

"Not the arm, really," Clint said, holding it up. "The hand. Your doctor says he thinks he can fix it."

"He probably can," Kane said. "Shale was a surgeon back East. Some woman broke his heart and he came here— or ended up here—to . . . hide, I guess. He's a really good doctor. I bet he can fix you."

"Oh, Clint . . ." Rosemary said.

"How many places are there in town to have breakfast?" Clint asked.

"This time of the morning, just one," Kane said, "Clara's Café, down the street. That big man, he was with two others. They might be there."

"They might," Clint said.

"If you don't mind," Kane said, "I'll come along. With your left hand, I don't think you'd be a match for three of them."

"Can you use that gun, Deputy?"

"I'm not very experienced," Kane admitted, "but the sheriff says I'm a natural."

"A natural, huh? Well, okay, then. Come on along. After all, it's your job."

"I suppose," Kane said, "I could just stand by and arrest the winner, but I'd rather back you."

FORTY-FOUR

Clint, Rosemary, and Deputy Kane walked over to Clara's Café.

"Wait," Clint said just before they entered the restaurant.

"What?" Kane asked.

"If the men are in there, I don't want to take Rosemary in," Clint said. "It's too dangerous."

"What do you want me to—" Rosemary started.

"Go back to the hotel," Clint said. "Go to your room until I come for you."

"And what if you don't come?" she asked.

"Don't worry, I'll come," he said.

"Clint—"

"Go, Rosemary," he said. "If I have to worry about you, that's when I could end up getting killed. Understand?"

"He's right, ma'am," Kane said. "You should go."

Rosemary hesitated, then said, "All right. But as soon as it's over, you come and get me."

"Agreed," Clint said.

She kissed him and said, "Be careful."

"Right."

As she walked away Kane said, "Pretty woman."

"Yes, she is." Clint looked at the deputy. He didn't usually go into any kind of gun action with someone unless he knew they truly could watch his back. He didn't know anything about this young man. "You ready, Deputy?"

"I'm ready, Mr. Adams."

Together, they entered the café.

Dillon and Quentin had just sat down with Raymond, who was already eating, when the door opened and Clint Adams walked in with the Clear Creek's deputy.

Clint saw the big man seated at a table and asked Kane, "Is that him?"

"Yes, sir, that's him."

Clint stared at the man, was wondering if he should approach him or wait when the man locked eyes with him.

He made his decision, and walked over to the man.

"Clint Adams," he said. "What's your name?"

"Dillon," the big man said without standing.

"I'm assuming you and your men tracked me here?" Clint asked.

"Why would we do that?" Dillon asked.

"You tell me."

Dillon stared at Clint for a few moments, then said, "I guess I don't have to. In here, or outside?"

"Too many innocent bystanders in here."

"Then on the street," Dillon said.

"I'm curious," Clint said. "You heard about my injury, didn't you?"

"What injury?"

Clint grinned. "Yeah, you did."

Dillon looked at Clint's gun.

"Wearin' for a cross draw?"

"Sure," Clint said. "I like to use my left hand every so often."

Dillon stood up.

"Should we go?"

His friends stood up, too.

"You boys stay where you are," Kane said. "We're gonna wait right here."

Quentin and Raymond exchanged a glance, then looked at Dillon.

"Order me some eggs," Dillon said. "I'll be right back."

The two men sat back down. Dillon went out the door, with Clint behind him.

Outside, Clint and Dillon stepped into the street.

"You've probably done this a lot in your life," Dillon said.

"Enough."

"Waitin' for the time you'll run into somebody faster? Better?"

"Better, maybe," Clint said. "Not necessarily faster."

"Faster is better," Dillon said.

Clint grinned. "We'll see."

Dillon backed away, to put some distance between them. He looked around, saw two or three people watching them.

"Fast, are you?" Clint asked.

"Fast enough," Dillon said.

It was clear to Clint that Dillon was the kind of man who thought speed was everything. That was bound to work in Clint's favor.

"Don't usually see gunmen with hands as big as yours," Clint said.

"You can't distract me, Adams," Dillon said. "This gun is made especially to fit my hand."

"Very nice."

"Sure you wanna cross draw like that?"

"I have to," Clint said. "I can't use my right hand."

"Can't use it?"

Clint held his arm up, his hand hanging limply from the end.

"Useless," Clint said.

Dillon's eyebrows went up. He was surprised Clint was admitting the injury.

"Puts you at a little bit of a disadvantage, don't it?" he asked.

Clint grinned. "That's the only reason you tracked me, isn't it?" Clint asked. "Figured I was helpless?"

"Too much talk, Adams," Dillon said. "Let's get this over with."

"Go ahead," Clint said.

Dillon went for his gun. He was right, he was fast.

Clint reached across his body, plucked his gun from his holster, taking his time.

Dillon fired first, and missed. He hit Clint, clipping the point of his shoulder, but he missed anything vital. As he moved to adjust, Clint calmly fired, putting a bullet dead center in the man's big chest.

"Wha—" Dillon said.

"Speed's not everything, Dillon," Clint said. "You've got to hit your target with the first shot—and make it a fatal hit."

He looked at his shoulder, where a little bit of blood was soaking into his shirt. By the time he looked back at Dillon, the big man was falling backwards.

Kane came running out, with Raymond and Quentin behind him. They stopped short when they saw Dillon lying on the ground.

"You boys better get your friend off the street," Kane said. "Unless you're not done?"

"No, no," Quentin said, "we're done."

Raymond and Quentin stepped into the street, reached down to Dillon, then looked up at Kane and asked, "Can we get some help?"

Kane looked over at the small crowd that had gathered and said, "You men, come over and help."

FORTY-FIVE

The doctor came out into the office from his surgery and looked at the five women gathered there.

"How is he?" Rosemary asked.

"How did it go?" Jenny asked.

"Is it over?" Abigail asked. "Can we go?"

"Shut up, Abigail," Morgan said.

"The surgery is over," Doctor Shale said. "As I suspected, there was a tendon that had been severed by the wagon when it punctured his arm."

"What did you do?" Rosemary asked.

"I repaired the tear."

"Will he be able to move his arm?" Jenny asked.

"And his hand?" Rosemary asked.

"His arm, yes," Shale said, "considering he was already able to do that. His hand . . . we'll have to see. I stitched the wound and bandaged it again."

"Is he awake?"

"No," Shale said. "When the ether wears off, he'll wake

up and we'll see. He won't be able to move the hand completely, but if he can even twitch his fingers, it will be a good sign."

"Can we wait?" Rosemary asked.

"That's what we're all gonna do," Doctor Shale said. "Wait."

About an hour later, they all crowded into the surgery as Clint came to.

"Hello," Doc Shale said. "How are you feelin'?"

"Groggy."

"Your friends are all here."

"Hey, everybody," Clint said to Rosemary, Jenny, and the rest.

"They'll all get out of here and let you rest, as soon as you move even one finger of your right hand."

"Can I?"

"That's what we want to see."

Clint looked down at his hand.

"Go ahead," Shale said. "Move it."

They all watched Clint's hand and then, suddenly, his index finger moved, and then his middle.

"That's it," Shale said. "Stop."

"I moved my hand," Clint said.

"Yes, you did," Shale said.

"It's going to be okay?"

"You'll need to exercise it, but there's every chance you'll get back full motion."

"How do I thank you?"

"Maybe I should thank you," Shale said. "Let's just thank each other."

Shale turned to the ladies. "Just a few minutes," he said, and left.

"I'll wait outside, too," Abigail said.

Jenny, Morgan, and Delilah all kissed Clint's cheek and said how glad they were he was going to be all right.

Rosemary took his left hand in hers.

"I'm so glad for you."

"Thank you, Rosemary," he said. "And thanks for being here."

"Clint, we have to leave."

"I figured as much."

"You need time to recover," she said, "and I owe it to the girls to take them to California."

"I understand. When are you leaving?"

"Today," she said. "Right now. We just wanted to wait 'til you woke up."

He squeezed her hand.

"Take care of yourself, and the girls."

"And you be careful," she said. "And do everything the doctor tells you."

"I swear."

She kissed him and left. Once he was alone, he looked down at this hand, moved his fingers again and then, with a lot of effort, made a loose fist.

He wouldn't have to perfect that cross draw after all.

Watch for

BITTERROOT VALLEY

355th novel in the exciting GUNSMITH series
from Jove

Coming in July!